Dear Romance Reader,

Welcome to a world of breathtaking passion and never-ending romance.
Welcome to *Precious Gem Romances*.

It is our pleasure to present *Precious Gem Romances*, a wonderful new line of romance books by some of America's best-loved authors. Let these thrilling historical and contemporary romances sweep you away to far-off times and places in stories that will dazzle your senses and melt your heart.

Sparkling with joy, laughter, and love, each *Precious Gem Romance* glows with all the passion and excitement you expect from the very best in romance. Offered at a great affordable price, these books are an irresistible value—and an essential addition to your romance collection. Tender love stories you will want to read again and again, *Precious Gem Romances* are books you will treasure forever.

Look for fabulous new *Precious Gem Romances* each month—available only at Wal★Mart.

Kate Duffy
Editorial Director

D1521492

Dear Bonjour Reader,

JINX &
TRACY

Sabrah H. Agee

Zebra Books
Kensington Publishing Corp.
http://www.zebrabooks.com

ZEBRA BOOKS are published by

Kensington Publishing Corp.
850 Third Avenue
New York, NY 10022

Copyright © 1999 by Sabrah H. Agee

Zebra and the Z logo Reg. U.S. Pat. & TM Off.

First Printing: September, 1999
10 9 8 7 6 5 4 3 2 1

Printed in the United States of America

For "Mama"

Sabrah Theodosia Enloe Huff
December 25, 1925-August 19, 1997

One

It was nearing midnight when Jenkins McGraw drove away from the hospital where she volunteered. She smiled as she remembered that her son, Jason, would be coming home for the weekend from military school. Her smile turned wry as she thought of the duffel bag of dirty laundry that he invariably brought with him.

"Darn," she muttered. "I'm out of detergent."

As she drove past a small shopping center, Jenkins noticed that the grocery store appeared to be open, so she pulled into the lot and parked near the store's entrance.

Jenkins pushed open the glass door, wondering where the cashiers were. There was no one standing at the line of registers near the front, though the lights were on and the doors unlocked. She walked farther into the store.

"Hello," she called. "Anybody here?" She waited a beat, but heard no reply. "Maybe they're all in the back," she mumbled, moving past the unmanned cash registers. She looked up at the large signs suspended over the aisles, spied the one that said *Detergents* and walked quickly toward it. As she started down the aisle, Jenkins noticed a man at the far end.

"Hi," she called. "I was beginning to think no one else was here."

His reply was a hoarse shout. "Run!"

Jenkins's step faltered. Run? As understanding finally registered, she spun on her heel to flee and found herself staring at the wrong end of a large pistol. On the other end was a man wearing a ski mask. He was hardly bigger than a young boy, but with that gun he might just as well have been ten feet tall.

"Drop the purse," the gunman ordered in a soft, almost feminine-sounding voice. Without hesitation, Jenkins shrugged off the strap of her shoulder bag and let it drop to the floor.

Keeping the pistol trained on her, the man picked up the purse and motioned for Jenkins to walk toward the back of the store. There, they joined another masked gunman and the man who'd shouted the warning. His hands were tightly bound with some kind of plastic cord.

"Are you all right?" the bound man asked, worry etching the handsomest face Jenkins had ever seen.

She nodded, "He took my purse, but I'm—"

"Shut up!" snapped the larger of the two gunmen. His voice was clearly masculine. "This ain't no social gatherin'." He looked at his partner, the little one whom Jenkins had begun to regard as "her" gunman, and growled, "Tie her up."

The smaller man ripped the cardboard wrapping off an extension cord and walked toward Jenkins. "Hold out your hands," he ordered. And when Jenkins complied, he said, "Just do what he says and he probably won't hurt you."

Probably? If he'd thought to reassure her, he'd

fallen somewhat short of the mark. As Jenkins looked into the eyes behind the slits in the ski mask, she realized there was something oddly familiar about them. Her musing was interrupted as he tightened the cord around her wrists.

Jenkins winced and was surprised when he murmured, "Sorry."

Bound securely, Jenkins and the other victim were led through a pair of swinging, stainless steel doors. Inside the area designated "Employees Only," the larger gunman strode over to a meat locker and yanked open the door. Then Jenkins and her unfortunate companion were shoved inside the small, cold room.

Several slabs of dressed meat were suspended from the ceiling and the gunman began looping a heavy, bright orange cord over the single empty hook. Jenkins watched anxiously as the other victim's bound wrists were fastened to the dangling end of the extension cord and his hands were hoisted over his head. Though the poor man's feet remained on the concrete floor, his big body was stretched taut.

Dread clawed at Jenkins's stomach and she squeaked with fright when she was grabbed from behind and lifted so that her tethered wrists could be looped over the bound man's head. While she dangled helplessly, the heavy cord hanging from the hook was also attached to her wrists. Thus, Jenkins was forced on tiptoe with her arms around the man's neck, her face pressing into his chest. She heard a heavy thud as the door to the meat locker was slammed shut, leaving them in total darkness.

"You can relax, they're gone," the man said.

With her arms wrapped securely around the

stranger's neck, Jenkins squirmed against his broad chest. Relax? She was hanging by her wrists, for God's sake! "Do you think they'll come back?"

"I doubt it." The man's deep baritone rumbled against her cheek. "They're probably long gone by now. If you'd only arrived five minutes later. . . ."

"We've got to figure a way to get out of here." She tugged at the cords binding her wrists, but only succeeded in making them tighter.

"Save your strength. There's no way we can get loose from these cords without help, so we'll just have to wait until someone finds us."

"But that could take forever!" Jenkins grimaced at the whine she heard in her voice, but she couldn't help herself. The cords were cutting into her wrists and her hands were growing numb.

"The police patrol this area fairly often." The stranger's voice was amazingly calm. "I'm sure the officers will notice the lights are still on and realize something's up."

"That'll be the day," Jenkins grumbled. "There's never a cop around when you need one." He laughed, and she frowned in the darkness. "Excuse me, but as we happen to be dangling from a hook in a meat locker, I find your jocularity a little odd."

"I was amused by your crack about the police."

"It wasn't meant to be funny."

"I know, but . . . allow me to introduce myself. I'm Detective R.D. Tracy, Birmingham P.D., Narcotics Division."

"You're a policeman?"

"I believe the term you used was cop."

Jenkins grimaced. Oh, great, she thought. I'm going to be hanging around with this man for God knows how long, and I've already insulted him. "Sorry. I didn't mean—"

"Forget it. I'm used to it. At least you didn't call us pigs."

Jenkins thought it best to change the subject. "So, why were you here when those men decided to rob this store?"

"The night manager's a friend and his wife just had a baby. It's my night off, so I was filling in for him. The store closes at midnight and I was about to lock up when they got the jump on me." He laughed without humor. "Then you walked in, and there was nothing I could do." He sighed. "Some cop I am."

"Don't blame yourself, Arty, it could've happened—"

"R.D.," he interrupted.

"Excuse me?"

"My name's not Arty, it's R.D. Tracy—short for Ross Dylan Tracy."

"So you're Detective Tracy?"

He sighed heavily. "Yes."

"I guess lots of people call you—"

"Ross," he interrupted. "I'm called Ross."

"I see." She made a mental note: No sense of humor. Great, just great. Growing more miserable by the minute, Jenkins squirmed, trying unsuccessfully to find a modicum of comfort.

"Put your legs around my waist."

Jenkins gasped indignantly. "I beg your pardon!"

"Don't get huffy. I'm not being fresh, I simply thought it might take some of the strain off your arms."

"Oh." Jenkins calmed down. His suggestion had

merit. After all, his feet were on the floor, but hers were barely touching it. And her hands were beginning to ache from the constriction. "Okay," she murmured, "I'll try."

She made several attempts, but she couldn't get her legs around him. Her straight skirt was half the problem, his height the other. "I can't do it," she groaned. "You're just too tall."

"Spread your legs," he ordered.

Jenkins swallowed nervously. "E-excuse me?"

"If I lift you on my knee, I think you'll be able to reach my waist."

"Oh." What was wrong with her? Why did everything the man said seem— She lost her train of thought and gasped in shock when his knee slipped between her legs.

"Easy," he murmured as he carefully raised his knee, and Jenkins, riding his muscular leg, felt her skirt creeping up her thighs as her toes left the floor.

"Can you reach my waist now?" he asked in a strained voice.

"Yes, I . . . think so. Yes." With her skirt no longer an impediment, Jenkins was able to straddle his waist. And Ross was right. The strain on her wrists and shoulders eased considerably.

"Better?" he asked a few seconds later.

"Y-yes, thank you." Jenkins, acutely aware that her skirt was hiked nearly to her waist, wondered he knew it. Then, without thinking, she murmured, "My Lord, you are huge."

He chuckled. "That's in my genes."

"Detective Tracy," Jenkins retorted, her voice dripping sarcasm, "When I said you were huge I wasn't referring to—"

He continued as if she hadn't spoken. "I'm six-four, my brother's six-six, my dad's six-three, and so was my granddad. Like I said, it's the Tracy genes."

"Ohhhh, you meant . . . never mind." Damn, his soft chuckle said he knew where her thoughts had strayed. Searching for something to say, Jenkins murmured, "It's cold in here."

"We *are* in a meat locker."

"Silly me. I hadn't noticed," she retorted. "It's easy to see why you became a detective. Your powers of observation are astounding."

He chuckled. "Are you always this funny?"

"Oh yeah, I'm a laugh a minute, especially when I'm in danger of becoming a human popsicle."

"Talk to me; it'll take your mind off things. What's your name?"

She sighed. "I'm Jenkins Jackson McGraw."

"Jenkins Jackson McGraw," he repeated. "Unusual name."

"Jackson's my maiden name."

"So, you're married?"

"Divorced," she replied. "Eighteen months ago my husband decided he preferred his twenty-two-year-old secretary to his wife. What about you?"

"I don't know, I've never seen his secretary."

"Very funny. Lucky for you that my hands are tied."

He laughed again. "I'm single and not looking to change my marital status."

"Smart man. Once was certainly enough for me. I don't—" Suddenly Jenkins felt something peculiar, a sort of buzzing at an extremely sensitive area of her anatomy and this strange buzzing seemed to be emanating from Detective Tracy. She gasped sharply. "What *are* you doing?"

Ross grunted. "Sorry. My pager's set to vibrate instead of sounding a beep."

"Oh!" Jenkins tried to move away from the vibration but it was impossible. Finally, it stopped.

"If that's Gilly, you might as well prepare for a few more calls."

She groaned. "How many more?"

"Well," he said ruefully. "My girlfriend has been known to page me five or six times before giving up. So, you might as well grin and enjoy it."

Jenkins sputtered. "Enjoy it?"

"Sorry, I only meant . . . I didn't think . . . sorry."

It must have been Gilly, because the pager soon began vibrating again. Detective Tracy apologized profusely and Jenkins wished he'd just shut up. The ordeal was embarrassing enough without his going on and on about it.

Jenkins had to endure three more pages before it finally stopped for good.

After several moments of silence, Jenkins muttered, "My nose is freezing."

"Put your face against my neck and it'll get warm."

The idea was tempting, but still, the thought of doing it seemed so . . . intimate. But her nose really was cold, so Jenkins hesitantly pressed her face against his warm neck.

Oh my God, she thought, he smells divine! Then she felt something hard graze her temple. *What on earth?* "Do you wear an earring?"

"Yeah. It's part of the uniform—I work narcotics, remember?"

"Oh. I see what you mean." Jenkins struggled to

recall what he looked like. She remembered that he was tall and dark . . . and handsome, with special emphasis on the handsome. Her grandmother would have said he was as fine as frog's hair. She remembered that he had the bluest eyes she'd ever seen, and eyelashes so thick and black that they looked artificial. And his long dark hair was tied at his nape.

"The long hair, is that part of the uniform, too?"

"Yeah." Then, "Mind if I warm my nose on your neck?"

Under the circumstances, how could she refuse? "Go ahead." Jenkins shuddered when his cold nose touched the skin just under her ear.

"Sorry," he mumbled.

The warmth of his breath raised goosebumps on every inch of her skin and she felt her nipples tighten to hard pebbles. She tried to tell herself that it was only a normal reaction to the cold, but her chest was pressed firmly against his and there was nothing cold about it. It's fear, she thought. It has absolutely nothing to do with the fact that I'm pressed intimately against an extremely handsome, virile male with a body like a Chippendale dancer's.

"Yeah, right," she muttered.

"You say something?" His voice vibrated pleasantly against her neck.

"I was wondering if we'll be here all night," she said quickly, and hoped she sounded convincing.

"Good question. Could be." He nestled his face more firmly against her neck. "God, you smell good."

Jenkins swallowed. "S-so do you." Then she grinned to herself. Here they were hanging in a meat locker like sides of beef and they were talking like a couple of kids on a first date.

She felt his cheeks flex against her neck and she knew he'd grinned, too. Then he murmured, "I wish we had—" Whatever he was going to say was interrupted when the door to the locker swung open and the beam of a flashlight danced over them.

"Well, I'll be damned," came an amused voice from behind the beam of light. "C'mere, Joe! You gotta see this!"

Two

Jenkins sat in the back seat of the patrol car and rubbed her thumb over the red weal on her wrist. By focusing on her wrists, she could avoid looking at the handsome detective.

The whole night had been one embarrassment after another. It was bad enough that the two policemen discovered her with her skirt hiked to her waist and her legs wrapped around Detective Tracy. But even worse was the fact that once they were freed, she'd been so flustered that Detective Tracy had actually had to *ask* her to take her legs from around him. And not just once, but twice! She cringed at the memory of the policemen's grins.

Ross's large hand closed over hers and squeezed it gently. "You okay?"

She nodded. Then she noticed the deep grooves in his wrist where the cords had bitten into the skin. Until that moment she hadn't considered how painful it must have been for him to have his hands hoisted in the air for such a long time. "What about you?"

"I've been through worse."

The patrolman who'd discovered them spoke from the front seat. "Good thing me and Joe noticed the lights was on in that store and decided to check it out," he said. "You two mighta hung there three or four more hours before somebody found you."

Jenkins shuddered at the thought and Ross put his arm protectively around her. "Yeah, Ed," he replied, "I owe you and Joe one. I might even put you guys in for a citation."

"Oh, you don't have to do that, Ross. Just seeing you trussed up like a Thanksgiving turkey was reward enough for us." Then the officer caught Jenkins's gaze in the rearview mirror. "How'd you end up in this mess, little lady?"

Acutely aware of the weight of Ross's arm around her shoulders, Jenkins had to struggle to reply. "I was on my way home from the hospital and stopped by the store for a box of detergent."

"Hospital? You a nurse?" Ross asked.

Jenkins found she still couldn't look at him. So she looked at their clasped hands and shook her head. "I fondle babies."

"You do what?"

She glanced up and laughed at his stunned expression. "I volunteer at the neonatal unit at St. Agnes's. Neonatal experts believe that high-risk babies who are touched often are more apt to survive than those who receive little or no human contact. The nurses have their hands full, so volunteers like me come in to stroke and caress these babies."

"Never heard of such a thing."

"Oh, the program's been around a long time. And I do love working with those precious babies."

"Must be tough when one doesn't make it."

She sighed. "I haven't had to face that, yet. When and if I do, I'll probably fall to pieces."

Ross hugged her. "Nah, you'll handle it. You're tough."

Jenkins looked at the big clock on the wall. It was three in the morning. She'd been sitting in a folding chair for nearly half an hour while Ross spoke with the officers assigned to the robbery. While she waited, she took advantage of the opportunity to get a good look at Ross.

Detective Tracy really was the handsomest man she'd ever seen—on or off the movie screen. He was dressed in jeans and a blue chambray shirt that matched his incredible eyes.

Jenkins tilted her head, studying the small gold hoop in his ear. She'd always thought a man wearing an earring looked ridiculous, but on Ross it looked exotic.

She wondered how old he was. Twenty-five? Thirty? No more than thirty-five, she was certain. Jenkins sighed and wished fervently that she were ten years younger.

"They want to talk to you now," Ross said, taking her arm to help her from the chair. The gesture irritated Jenkins. His solicitude drove home the difference in their ages.

Ross introduced her to Lieutenant Chuck Llewellyn.

"Thank you for being so patient, Ma'am," the investigating officer said. "I expect Ross told us all there is to tell, but I thought I'd ask if you could think of anything that might help us."

Jenkins started to say that she could think of nothing else, when she suddenly remembered her assailant's eyes. "You know, I think I may know one of them. In fact, I may know both of them."

"What?" Ross and the lieutenant spoke simultaneously.

"I just remembered that my gunman—well, not mine, exactly, but the one who held a gun on me—seemed familiar. And I now realized why."

The lieutenant pointed to a chair. "Have a seat, Mrs. McGraw, and tell me what you think you know."

Jenkins sat. "I volunteer in a neonatal unit at St. Agnes Hospital," she began.

"She fondles babies," a grinning Ross interjected.

"She what?"

He gave her a conspiratorial wink. "I'll explain later. Go on, Jinx."

Jenkins smiled up at Ross. He'd called her "Jinx" and for some silly reason the nickname pleased her enormously

"Mrs. McGraw? You were saying?"

She reluctantly dragged her gaze back to the lieutenant. "As I was saying, I work in a neonatal unit—"

"Fondling babies," the lieutenant said dryly.

"Yes. A couple of weeks ago a new baby was brought into the unit. The mother was still in her teens, a cocaine abuser. The baby was underweight and, of course, addicted to crack, too."

"What has this got to do with—"

"I'm trying to tell you that I'm almost certain that my gunman was that baby's mother," she said.

"I thought both the gunmen's faces were masked?"

"They were, but I think I recognized her voice, and I saw her eyes. They were very unusual. The gunman has one green eye and one brown eye, same as the crack baby's mother."

The lieutenant looked at Ross. "What do you think, Tracy? Could one of the gunmen have been a woman?"

"Sure. I told you that one was a little guy."

The lieutenant snorted. "Compared to you, Tracy, everybody's a little guy." He looked back at Jenkins. "You said you thought you knew both assailants?"

"Yes, though I can't be certain because I only saw him once. I think the other one is the baby's father."

"Can you describe him?"

She closed her eyes as she tried to recall the man she'd seen at the hospital. "He's Caucasian, in his late twenties or early thirties. His hair is cropped close and he's approximately six-three, maybe six-four. I can't even guess his weight, but he was well built—like someone who works out with weights. I remember that he had a tattoo on the top of his hand. It looked homemade, was crudely drawn, but I can't remember what it was."

"Do you know his name?"

"No."

He made some notes, then looked up at her. "What about the girl?"

"She's blonde, fair complexioned, about seventeen." Jenkins shook her head sadly. "The poor thing's terribly thin, hardly more than skin and bones."

"In other words, she looks like a crackhead."

"I suppose. I only know it broke my heart to see her."

"Know her name?"

"It was Jenny, no . . . no, it wasn't Jenny, but it was something like Jenny." She tapped her chin. "Oh, I know, it was Ginger. Ginger Graham. I remember that her boyfriend called her 'Gigi.' " She looked at the lieutenant. "That's all I know. But you can probably get more from the hospital records."

The lieutenant closed his notebook. "I'm sorry you had to go though this, Mrs. McGraw, but you've been a big help." He picked up the phone. "I'll have someone take you home now."

"I'll take her home," Ross said. "You just get somebody to see that her car gets there."

The lieutenant shook his head. "Sorry, Ross, but I'll need you at the scene."

Jenkins spoke up. "Listen, I'm fine, I can drive. Just take me back to my car and I can get myself home, all right?"

The lieutenant shrugged. "Okay by me. You can ride to the store with Ross since he's going anyway."

They started out the door when Ross grimaced. "My pager's vibrating." He unclipped it from his belt and read the lighted numbers. "Wait just a second, and I'll be right back."

Jenkins watched Ross hurry into an empty office and pick up a telephone receiver. A moment later he spoke into it. Then he glanced up at Jenkins, winked and smiled, and turned his back to lean against the edge of the desk.

Jenkins sighed and looked at her watch. Four o'clock and she was very tired. Just then the patrolman who'd rescued them walked by. "Ed?" she said hesitantly.

He looked up and grinned. "Well, hey, Mrs. McGraw. You still here?"

"I'm afraid so. Detective Tracy was about to take me back to my car, but he seems to be tied up. Would you mind giving me a lift?"

Ed glanced in the office at Ross on the telephone. "Must be the girlfriend of the moment," he muttered. "I don't know how he keeps up with all of them." Ed shook his head. "Forget I said that." Then he smiled and took her arm. "Come on, Miz McGraw, I'll be glad to give you a lift to your car."

Jenkins climbed out of the patrol car. "Thank you for the lift, Ed, and for rescuing me from the meat locker."

Ed grinned. "Anytime, Miz McGraw. It was all in a day's work."

As Ed drove away, Jenkins noticed the yellow tape that bore the words *Crime Scene—Do Not Enter* around the entrance to the store. "Darn," she muttered. "And I still don't have any detergent." She looked up as a bright red sports car with darkly tinted windows sped into the parking lot and slid to a stop a few feet from her. She was about to scream for help when the car door opened and Ross stepped out.

Jenkins clutched at her throat. "You scared me to death!"

"Why didn't you wait for me?" he asked, striding toward her.

"You were busy and Officer Patches offered me a lift." She shrugged. "Why? Was there something else you wanted from me?"

He seemed about to say something. Then he looked around, shifted his feet, and mumbled, "I just wanted to say good-bye."

"Oh. Well. . . ." She stuck out her hand. "Good-bye, Detective Tracy. I must say, meeting you has been quite an experience."

He took her hand and held it for a moment. Then he smiled crookedly. "Same here," he said. "If there's ever anything I can do for you, you only have to ask."

"Actually, there is something you can do for me."

"Name it."

"You can go though that yellow tape and get a box of detergent for me." She rolled her eyes and grinned. "You'd think after hanging around the store all that time I would have remembered why I went there in the first place."

He laughed. "What brand?"

"Kleen," she said, "with bleach."

"I'll just be a minute." Then he stepped over the yellow tape and strode into the store.

Jenkins sighed as she watched him walk away. Then she leaned against the fender of her car and thought for a moment. If she were younger or if he were older she would. . . . She shook her head. She'd what? Go after him?

Jenkins closed her eyes. A man like Ross Tracy could have any woman he wanted by just crooking his little finger. A man like Ross Tracy wouldn't give a woman like Jenkins McGraw a second glance. And even if he did, Jenkins knew from experience that her teenage son would do his best to put a wrench in the works. "But I can wish," she murmured.

"And your wish is my command."

Jenkins opened her eyes to find Detective Tracy leaning over her. "Oh!" she stammered and scrambled to stand upright.

"Sorry, I didn't mean to startle you. Here's your detergent." He held up the big green box decorated with a spiral of yellow, red, and orange. "See? Kleen, with bleach." When she didn't say anything, he frowned. "What's the matter? Isn't this what you wanted? I can take it back and—"

"No! No, you're exactly—I mean—*that* is exactly what I wanted." She took the box from him. "Thank you." She turned and unlocked her car door and then looked back at him. "Thanks for everything, Ross."

He lightly touched her chin with his fist. "No problem."

She got into the car and when he tapped on the window she rolled it down. "You be careful driving home," he said.

"Thanks, I will."

"Hey, Jinx?"

"Yes?"

He seemed about to say something else, and then he shook his head. "Never mind."

She turned the key and the car engine sprang to life. "Well, I guess I'll be going."

Ross gripped the door and stuck his head inside the car and kissed her lightly on the cheek. "Take care, Jinx." Then he stepped back and motioned for her to leave.

With a last look at his handsome face, Jenkins rolled up the window and slowly drove out of the parking lot. As she pulled out onto the street, she glanced in the rearview mirror and saw he was still standing where she'd left him, watching.

Three

Jason had arrived home at seven o'clock to dump his usual load of dirty laundry. He'd listened while his mother told him what had happened last night, mumbled a few "no kiddings," and then announced that he was going to visit his girlfriend.

The moment Jason left, Jenkins had called her best friend Tish Armstrong. Now, still in her pajamas, Jenkins described her adventure to her friend. And Tish paid attention to the tale, especially the part about her legs being wrapped around Detective Tracy's waist.

Tish sighed when Jenkins finished the tale. "That's the most incredible story I've ever heard. That detective, what was his name?"

"Ross Dylan Tracy. He's called Ross."

"And he was really good-looking?"

Jenkins leaned back and closed her eyes. "I'm telling you, he was the best looking man I've ever seen."

"Come on," Tish said, her tone doubtful. "Better than Mel?"

"It's hard to believe, but he looks better than Mel Gibson."

Tish stood up. "Come on, get your clothes on."

"Why? Where are we going?"

Hands on her hips, Tish arched a brow at Jenkins. "Down to the police station. I've got to see this cop for myself."

"You're nuts! I'm not going to the police station."

"Guess I'll have to wait till you two start dating."

Jenkins rolled her eyes. "Tish, he's no more than thirty-five years old and he looks like a movie star."

Tish rested her chin on her hand. "So?"

"So he won't be asking *me* out."

"Why wouldn't he?" Tish countered.

"For one thing, I'm too old for him."

"You're only thirty-nine."

"I'll be forty next week. He wouldn't be interested in me."

Tish frowned at her friend. "And why not? You're a great looking woman, Jenkins. You're smart, you're funny, and most women would kill to have your figure."

"Let's not forget my skin," Jenkins said cynically. "I dare say most women would just love to look like a speckled hen."

"So you have a few freckles—"

"A few? Tish, every square inch of my skin looks like a page from one of those Connect-the-Dots books."

"Your boobs and your butt aren't freckled," she retorted.

"I thought we were discussing the parts of my body that people can see," Jenkins said dryly.

"So what? Most people think freckles are cute."

"On little kids, maybe. But not on middle-aged women. It's a moot point, anyway. Even if by some miracle the detective were interested, Jason would never accept my going out with him."

"Sooner or later Jason is going to have to understand that you and his father are finished. This fantasy about y'all being a family again isn't healthy for him and it isn't fair to you."

Jenkins nodded and rubbed her temples. "I know, I know you're right about Jason. And I've tried to make him see the way things are, but he refuses to acknowledge any of it. And as for the other, well, even if Jason weren't a problem, after all I've been through in the past two years, the last thing I want is some man to complicate my life. And you know, having lived with Jake for fifteen years, I've found that being single isn't so bad."

Tish sighed. "Sometimes I'd like to take a stick and beat the hell out of Jake McGraw."

Jenkins raised a brow. "What brought that on?"

"Because your ex-husband has singlehandedly made you leery of any 'body' that happens to have muscles and a hairy chest."

Jenkins laughed. "When you consider that I was dumped by one who promised to love and honor me till death, can you blame me?"

"No. But it just burns me that the jerk can still influence you. I could just wring his big, old, ugly, red neck."

Jenkins grinned at her friend. "If you're waiting for me to talk you out of it, you've got a long wait ahead of you."

They were laughing when Jason sauntered into the kitchen. "What's so funny? I could hear you two from out in the garage. You sounded like a couple of cackling hens."

"Funny you should say that, Jason." Tish winked

at Jenkins. "Your mom and I were just discussing an old rooster."

"What?"

Jenkins shot her friend a stern look as she stood up and hugged her son. "We were being silly. Want some breakfast?"

"I'd love some bacon and eggs."

"Coming right up."

"Considering what your mom's been through in the past few hours, don't you think you could fix your own breakfast, Jason?"

"Tish!"

"Jenkins, you haven't had more than two hours' sleep. Jason knows how to fry an egg. They teach him survival skills in military school, don't they?"

"Well, yeah, but—" Jason was about to brag about everything he'd learned, but suddenly thought better of it.

"As a matter of fact, I'll bet good old Jason will even fix his mom's breakfast for a change? Right, Jason?"

Jason sighed. "Yeah, mom, I'll fix breakfast."

"Oh, Jason, are you sure?"

Tish grabbed Jenkins by the arm. "Of course he's sure. He's a big boy. Now sit before you fall down. Good Lord, woman, you're dead on your feet."

Jenkins eased back in her chair. "Well, I am a little tired. All the excitement, I guess."

Grinning, Tish leaned over and whispered, "Spending a couple of hours with my legs wrapped around a handsome man would wear *me* out."

Jenkins laughed out loud. "Tish, you're awful! What would Buzzy say if he heard you?"

"Buzzy stopped being shocked by me years ago—
he knew the job was dangerous when he took it."

"Buzzy wouldn't change a hair on your head."

She smiled. "Yeah, I know. Buzzy has good taste
and that's why I adore him." Tish stood up. "You
need to get some sleep, so I'd better go. Let me know
when you get that call."

"What call?"

"The one from Dick Tracy, of course."

"It's *Ross* Tracy and he isn't going to call."

Just then the phone rang and Jason answered it.
"Hello? Yeah, she's here, just a minute. Mom, telephone for you."

"Who is it?" she mouthed.

"Somebody with the police department."

Tish gasped. "I knew it!" she whispered excitedly.
"It's that detective!" She gave Jenkins a little shove.
"Go on, answer it."

In spite of her insistence that Ross wasn't going
to call, and in spite of the fact that she had no desire
to go out with anyone, Jenkins's heart did a little
flip-flop when she took the phone from Jason.

"H-hello? This is Jenkins McGraw." But when she
heard the voice on the other end, her heart fell.
"Oh, hi, Lieutenant Llewellyn."

"Darn!" Tish muttered.

Jason walked over to his mother's friend. "What's
going on? Who'd you think was on the phone?"

"Nobody important," Tish replied.

Jenkins finished her conversation and hung up
the phone. "Well, Jason, you can forget about fixing
my breakfast. I've got to go back down to the police
station."

"What for?"

"They've picked up a couple of suspects and want me to see if I can identify them."

Jason shrugged and went back to preparing his own breakfast. Tish, on the other hand, grabbed Jenkins's arm and pulled her into the next room. "Will *he* be there?"

Jenkins rolled her eyes. "I don't know, the lieutenant didn't say. I suppose it's possible."

"Then I'm going with you," she declared.

"You're what?"

"I'm going with you. You're entirely too exhausted to drive yourself and I want to get a gander at this hunk in uniform." She folded her hands under her chin. "Please, Jenkins, let me go with you."

Jenkins laughed. "Oh, all right. You can drive me—*if* you promise to behave yourself. And Ross doesn't wear a uniform, Tish, he's a detective. And there's no guarantee he'll be there."

"But he might be. I'll be back in two shakes."

"Where are you going?"

"To change clothes, of course. I can't be introduced to an undercover Adonis in these old things." She started to the door and paused to look back at Jenkins. "Wear your cashmere, Jenkins, you look marvelous in cashmere."

"Don't be ridiculous."

"Oh, all right. But wear the camel coat. It makes your hair look like polished copper."

"It's nearly seventy degrees outside. I will not be wearing a coat."

"Honestly, Jenkins, you're no fun at all," Tish replied petulantly.

"Isn't that what I've been telling you all morning?"

* * *

Jenkins studied the women in the line up. "That's Ginger Graham," she said, "second from the left."

The lieutenant nodded. "Okay, that wraps it up. By the way, we found your purse in her apartment. It's in my office. You can get it while you're here, if you'd like. Just tell Sergeant Suddeth I said he can release it to you today."

"Thank you, Lieutenant." Jenkins replied. "What's going to happen to Ginger now?"

"She'll be charged with robbery, but since she's young and this is her first offense, she'll probably get a light sentence."

"And her boyfriend?"

The lieutenant frowned. "He's another matter altogether. Ray Price has a record a mile long. If we ever catch him—"

"You mean he's still out there somewhere?" This came from Tish.

"Yes ma'am, but we'll get him."

"Jenkins," Tish said worriedly. "That man knows you. You could be in danger." She looked pointedly at the lieutenant. "Sir, I think you should assign someone to watch over Jenkins, and I think you should assign Detective Tra—"

Jenkins clamped her hand over Tish's mouth. "Excuse my friend, Lieutenant. Tish gets overly excited when she forgets to take her medicine." She started dragging the muzzled woman toward the door. "Come along, Tish, so everyone can get back to work."

Jenkins pulled Tish out into the hall. "I'm going to strangle you with my bare hands if you don't stop!" she whispered. She wanted to be angry, but it was so hard to be angry with someone like Tish.

Tish shrugged. "I thought it was a good idea."

"Well, I didn't."

"Is that you, Jinx?"

Even if she hadn't heard the familiar voice, Jenkins would have known who was behind her. The glazed look in Tish's eyes as she looked over Jenkins's shoulder all but shouted his name. She took a deep breath and turned to face him.

"Hi, Detective Tracy, I didn't expect to see you after last night. Don't you ever rest?"

He grinned and Jenkins felt her heart skip at least three beats. "I could ask you the same. Have you seen the line up?"

She nodded. "It was Ginger Graham. The lieutenant said they found my purse in her apartment. I was on my way to pick it up."

Tish elbowed her in the ribs. "All right, Tish!" She looked apologetically at Ross. "Detective Ross Tracy, may I introduce my dearest friend, Tish 'The Relentless' Armstrong."

Tish stepped forward. "I'm delighted to meet you, Detective. I must say you're everything Jenkins said you were."

Ross arched a brow at Jenkins. "Oh?"

"I told her you were very tall." She glowered at Tish. "Isn't that *right*, Tish?"

"What? Oh. Yes. Tall. Jenkins said you were really tall, and I see that she was right." She cocked her head. "By the way, Detective, how old are you?"

"Tish! For God's sake!"

Ross chuckled. "I'm thirty-seven, why?"

Tish looked at Jenkins with an I-told-you-so expression and said, "I was just wondering."

Jenkins grabbed Tish's arm. "We've got to be going."

"I was sort of hoping we could go for a cup of coffee."

"That's a great idea!" Tish, again.

"Thanks, Ross, but I'm really exhausted." Then Jenkins glanced at Tish and narrowed her eyes. "Besides, I've got to get this one back to her cell before they realize she's escaped."

Ross laughed. "Then how about a rain check?"

This time her smile was genuine. "Perhaps," she said. She started down the hall with Tish in tow.

"Hey, Jinx?"

She looked back at him. "Yes?"

He grinned. "You still smell great."

She flushed. "Thanks," she murmured and, purposefully ignoring Tish's arch look, she headed toward the exit.

Tish smiled wickedly and said in an all-too-clear voice, "You were right, Jenkins, he *is* better-looking than Mel Gibson."

Four

Following the maitre d', Jenkins threaded her way through the dining room and smiled warmly when her dinner companion rose to pull out her chair. "Sorry I'm late, Douglas. Have you been waiting long?"

Dr. Douglas Champion, one of Birmingham's most successful internists, gave Jenkins an obligatory kiss on the cheek and said in his slow drawl, "Not too long. I timed my arrival fifteen minutes later than we'd arranged to meet."

"How clever of you," she said, laughing. "In any case, it was sweet of you to invite me to dinner tonight."

"Well, it *is* your birthday after all, and I couldn't bear the thought of your doing nothing to celebrate." He nodded to the waiter. "I've ordered champagne."

As the waiter poured the champagne Jenkins watched the golden liquid fizz and bubble. Then she arched a brow at Douglas. "You probably shouldn't have done this. Two glasses of champagne and my speech begins to slur. Three and there's a distinct possibility that I'll start dancing on tables."

He waved his hand as if shooing a fly. "So dance, dahlin', it's your birthday."

She sighed. "If you want to know the truth, I'd just as soon forget my birthday."

Douglas lowered his chin and pursed his lips. "Jenkins, turning forty isn't the end of the world, you know."

"Maybe not, but it feels like it."

"Then let's talk about something else. I've been dying to hear all about your adventure the other night. Tell me all the details, especially the ones about your detective."

Jenkins grinned. "You've been talking to Tish, haven't you?"

"But of course." He leaned forward and lowered his voice. "She says he's divine, an absolute god."

She took a deep swallow of the champagne. "He is special."

Douglas wiggled a brow. "Should I be interested?"

"If you're asking if he's gay, I don't think so." Then she laughed, remembering the incident of the pager. "No, I'm certain he's straight."

"I see. So, is there a romance blossoming between you two?"

Jenkins traced the rim of her glass with her finger. "No, absolutely not."

"And why not?"

"Douglas, I'm just getting my life back on track and I don't need any complications. Jason hasn't been able to accept that it's over between his dad and me, so right now a romantic involvement with any man would be impossible. Besides, Ross Tracy's much too young." She shrugged, "Or I'm too old. Take your pick."

"Dahlin', don't be ridiculous, there's no such thing as too young or too old—assuming, of course, that he's past the age of consent."

Jenkins laughed. "Rest assured, Douglas, he's definitely past the age of consent."

"Well then?"

"He's still younger than I."

"So what?"

"It makes a difference."

"Why?"

"It just does, that's all—" She paused at the irritating beep of Douglas's pager.

He took the small instrument out of his pocket and glanced at the lighted digits. Then he motioned to a waiter. "Telephone, please." He smiled wryly. "Sorry, dahlin', occupational hazard."

"I understand."

The waiter brought the telephone to the table and Douglas quickly dialed the number. "This is Dr. Champion." He listened for a moment, nodded and said, "Tell them I'll be there in ten minutes." He hung up the phone and sighed deeply. "That was my service. It seems that one of my patients is having a gallbladder attack, so I must fly. I'm so sorry."

"Perfectly all right. I appreciate your remembering my birthday even if we did have to cut the evening short."

Douglas stood up. "Don't you leave because I must. Stay and order whatever your heart desires, Jenkins."

"You may be sorry you're being so generous."

"Never, dahlin'. It's only money." And with a kiss near her cheek, he was gone.

Jenkins sighed and leaned back in her chair. Some birthday party, she thought morosely. Without waiting for the waiter to serve her, she lifted the champagne bottle from the ice bucket and refilled her glass. She'd already drunk two glasses and didn't feel even the slightest bit tipsy. Maybe, at the ripe old age of forty, she had finally developed a tolerance to alcohol.

The red sports car moved slowly down the street, its darkly tinted windows obliterating any suggestion as to the identity of its occupants. Detective Ross Tracy and his partner, Detective Kelly O'Brian, scanned the nearly empty streets watching for signs of drug deals going down. Both men were tired. In a few minutes their shift would be over and they were looking forward to going to their respective homes and getting some sleep.

"Uh-oh," Kelly said, nodding toward a parking lot. "We've got a DUI in the making."

"Where?" Ross asked.

Kelly chuckled and nodded toward a late model BMW. "Over there, the chick in the brown dress with the gorgeous legs. Unless I miss my guess, she's as drunk as Cooter Brown."

Ross craned his neck to see over the hedge ringing the parking area. Then, as Kelly drove the car into the parking lot, he spotted her. She appeared to be trying to unlock her car, but was having difficulty getting the key in the lock. And judging from the way she swayed and staggered, she was more than a little inebriated. Her hair hid her face until she pushed the red, shoulder-length tresses behind her ear.

"Holy Christ!" Ross muttered when he got a clear view.

Kelly glanced at him. "What's the matter?"

Ross reached for the door latch. "Do me a favor, buddy?"

"Sure."

"Just drop me off here and go on home."

Kelly looked at his partner. "You sure about this?"

Ross stared at the woman who'd haunted his dreams for over a week. He nodded. "Yeah, I'm sure."

Kelly looked at the woman again. "You know her?"

"Oh, yeah," he murmured as he opened the door. "I know her." He unfolded himself from the interior of the sports car, got out, and waved as his partner sped away. Shaking his head, Ross headed for the woman.

"Jinx?" he said, walking up behind her. She whirled around and staggered against the door of her car.

She cupped her hand over her eyes and squinted at his face. "Ross?" She hiccupped. "Z'at you?"

"Nobody else," he replied. "I see you've been celebrating."

She straightened and raised her chin a notch. "*Hic.* H-how did y-you know?"

"A lucky guess." He couldn't help grinning at her obvious attempt to appear sober.

Then she slumped and grinned back at him. "It's my, um, birthday, you know. *Hic!*" She frowned and put her hand on her throat. Her expression was confused, as if she couldn't fathom where the hiccups were coming from.

"Happy birthday."

"Thanks. I—*hic*—reached the big Four-Oh today."

"Congratulations."

Her face crumpled into a frown. "I don't want to be forty." She put her hands over her face and began to slide.

Ross grabbed her under the arms and propped her against the fender. He took the car keys from her limp hand. "Why don't I drive you home, Jinx?"

She peered up at him. "Ross, is that really you?"

He chuckled. "In the flesh, sweetheart."

"I didn't just dream you up?"

"Nope. I'm really here."

She smiled crookedly. "I'm glad."

Grinning to himself, Ross walked her around to

the passenger side and opened the door. "I'm going to drive you home, okay?"

She grinned and tapped him on the chest. "Okee dokee, artichokee." She giggled as he eased her into the passenger seat and buckled her seat belt. Then he hurried to the driver's side and got in. He turned the key and listened a moment to the engine's purr.

"Okay, Jinx, what's your address?" When she didn't answer, he looked at her. "Jinx?" He turned on the interior light and saw that her eyes were closed. Ross shook her gently, but she was out cold. "Oh, Christ," he muttered.

He opened her evening bag, hoping to find something with her address on it. Nothing there but a lipstick and a little mirror.

He closed his eyes. Now what? He looked at her again and saw that she had turned slightly to nestle her cheek against her hand. Forty years old and she looked like a kid. He reached over and pushed a lock of hair behind her ear.

"Well, Jinx, I guess you'll just have to go home with me."

Wondering if he weren't making the biggest mistake of his life, Ross shifted the car into drive and headed toward home.

Five

Jenkins blinked and frowned at the annoying ray of sunlight that had managed to find its way between the slats of the miniblinds. She smacked her lips and grimaced at the dark brown taste, idly wondering what creature had died in her mouth.

She pushed herself up and groaned aloud when a sharp pain pierced her brain. Then moving slowly so as not to jostle her aching head, Jenkins sat up and eased her feet to the floor. She rested her throbbing head in her hands and struggled to recall exactly what she had done to warrant such utter misery.

Ah yes, the birthday celebration. She remembered meeting Douglas, remembered drinking champagne, remembered that Douglas was called out to see a patient. But, for the life of her, she couldn't remember anything else. At least nothing cohesive. There were flashes, a kaleidoscope of images too fleeting to register in her fuzzy brain. She swallowed back the bile that threatened to add further insult to her already rancid tongue.

Sitting on the edge of the bed with her head between her hands, Jenkins opened her eyes and stared at the floor. She blinked at the brown carpet under her bare feet.

Brown?

The carpet in her bedroom was green, moss green. Slowly, she raised her head and let her gaze drift upward to the beige walls and the brown and green plaid curtains. Her bedroom didn't have beige walls. Her bedroom walls were creamy white and her pale yellow draperies were adorned with sweetheart roses. Hangover or no hangover, she knew that this was *not* her bedroom.

Jenkins looked to her right and recoiled when someone stared back. She almost giggled when she realized the "someone" was her own reflection.

Then, focusing her bleary, puffy eyes on her mirrored image, and seeing the mass of tangles sticking out at odd angles all over her head, she muttered, "I look like Medusa."

Suddenly Jenkins noticed she was wearing a very large pajama top that she'd never seen before. She fingered the fabric of the unfamiliar shirt and, swallowing nervously, she pulled out the shirt's neck and looked down it. Dear God in heaven, she didn't have a stitch on under there!

Out of the corner of her eye Jenkins saw something move and she turned to look. Horrified, she covered her eyes.

"Ohmygod-ohmygod-ohmygod," she chanted.

Peeking through her fingers, she prayed she'd been wrong and what she'd seen was a trick of the light. No, there was no mistaking the foot—a man's foot—which was connected at the ankle to a very long, very muscular, very hairy calf. Whose?

Still peeking through her fingers, she let her gaze travel up the calf to the bent knee that protruded from the sheet, past the knee to the thigh, across a swath of more sheet to a partially uncovered hip, up and over a broad, somewhat hairy chest, and finally to the man's face.

All the breath left her body in one heavy swoosh.

Ohmygod-ohmygod-ohmygod!

She closed her eyes. It wasn't possible that she had spent the night with Ross Tracy—was it? She glanced at him again.

Ohmygod-ohmygod-ohmygod.

How had this happened? What had she done? She looked in the mirror again and groaned inwardly. What hadn't she done? Jenkins mumbled a prayer and crossed herself—a movement which, considering her present circumstance, might have been prudent had she been a Roman Catholic. However, being a dyed-in-the-wool Presbyterian, the religious gesture drove home to her just how terribly confused she was.

She eased off the bed, stood up slowly, and waited for the world to stop teetering. She noticed a bathroom on the other side of the room so she tiptoed around the bed and into the bathroom, quietly closing the door behind her. She leaned against the door, closed her eyes, and tried to think what to do. Where was her car? And more importantly, how had she come to be with Ross Tracy?

"I can't think about that now," she muttered. "I've got to think about getting out of here." She took a deep breath, opened her eyes—and groaned. Her clothes were hanging over the shower rod. Her dress, her brand-new silk dress, was stained and wrinkled beyond belief. Beside it hung her slip, her bra, her pantyhose and—"Oh no!"

Her face flamed when she saw the thick, cotton, "old lady" panties draped over the rod. When she reached for them, she found they were damp. Why? Had it rained last night? Had she fallen in a swimming pool? Had she *jumped* into one? She drew in a deep breath.

"I don't even want to know," she muttered as she began donning the damp, clammy clothes.

Jenkins looked out the small window, hoping to see something familiar, anything that would tell her where she was so that she could call a taxi to come for her. She nearly wept with relief when she saw her car parked in the yard—she had a means of escape.

Dressed in her damp and wrinkled clothes, Jenkins eased open the bathroom door and peeked out. Ross was still sleeping soundly, thank God. Now, all she had to do was find her shoes, her purse, and her car keys.

She let her gaze traverse the room. She spied her evening bag on the bedside table. Of course, she thought wryly, it would be on the table farthest away. One shoe peeped from under the bed—the other was probably there, too. Now, for her car keys. She narrowed her eyes, searching, concentrating. There they were! Lying on the table next to Ross—barely three inches from his head! She decided it would be judicious to get them last.

She tiptoed toward the night stand and when she was almost there, she stubbed her toe on the metal leg of the bed. Tears sprang to her eyes, sweat dotted her brow, and she bit down hard on her knuckle to keep from screeching in pain. Oh, God, how much more abuse could she take? Finally, after first testing her weight on the toe, Jenkins limped to the night stand and retrieved her purse. One down, she mentally calculated.

Determined not to stub another toe, Jenkins dropped to her knees and crawled to the other side of the bed. She retrieved one sandal and felt around for the other but, except for several dust bunnies, she came up empty-handed. Then she stuck her head under the bed to look for the shoe, but only got a nose full of dust and a bump on her head for her trouble. She decided to forget the shoe and concentrate on getting the car keys.

She crawled to the bedside table and reached for the keys just as Ross turned over and flopped his arm off the side of the bed. His large hand conked Jenkins squarely in the middle of her face and for a moment, she saw stars. She sat back on her haunches and ran her fingers over her throbbing nose, half expecting to find it mashed as flat as a Pekinese pup's. It seemed to be all right, but tomorrow she would no doubt have at least one black eye—if not two. Great, she thought grimly. I'll look like I've been in a barroom brawl.

She tried once more and was able, finally, to snatch the keys off the night stand. Then, barefooted, her head pounding in rhythm with her racing heart, Jenkins tiptoed out of the room and down a back hall. Within moments she was inside her car. She turned the key in the ignition and let out a long sigh of relief when the engine purred with life.

Tish tapped on the back door and Jenkins opened it and then shuffled back to the table.

"Good Lord, Jenkins," Tish said as she followed her across the kitchen. "What happened to you?"

Jenkins sat down and propped her head in her hands. "I wish I knew," she murmured, as images of her damp clothes came to mind.

Tish sat across from her. "What's the matter?"

"Oh, Tish, I've probably done something really, really stupid."

Tish grinned. "You? Miss Always-Looks-Before-She-Leaps?" She wiggled in her seat. "I can't wait to hear this. I want all the details, so start at the beginning and don't leave anything out."

Jenkins raised her head and blinked at her friend. "Tish, I'm not kidding. This is serious."

Tish's smile faded. "What in the world happened? I thought you were going to celebrate your birthday with Douglas."

"I was. We arranged to meet at La Petite Fleur."

"Mon Dieu! La Petite Fleur is très chic and, ooh la la, très expensive," Tish quipped. Then, in a contrite tone, "Sorry, I got carried away. Go on."

"Douglas ordered champagne."

"Good for Douglas."

"Not good. Right after he ordered it he was called away on an emergency. So there I was, alone and feeling sorry for myself with a nearly full bottle of champagne staring me in the face." She sighed. "You know how champagne affects me, Tish."

"Oh, yeah, I'd forgotten." Then her friend's eyes widened. "Oh, dear, you didn't drink it all?"

"I think I must have—or at least a good portion of it."

"Uh-oh. Did you dance on the table?"

"No. At least I don't think so."

"Then, what happened?"

"I don't know. I remember saying goodnight to Douglas and the next thing I know I'm waking up in a strange room, in a strange bed, with—"

Tish gasped. "A strange man?"

"I woke up with a man, all right, but he wasn't exactly a stranger."

"Jenkins, don't tell me you ended up in bed with your ex! No wonder you're upset."

Jenkins shook her head. "It wasn't Jake, Tish. It was Ross Tracy."

Tish's eyes nearly bulged. "Are you saying that

you slept with the Better-than-Mel, the Twentieth-Century-Adonis, the Detective-Hunk-Extraordinaire?"

Jenkins nodded.

"I think I may die. Can envy kill a person?" She leaned over the table. "Look at my face, Jenkins. Do I look green to you?"

Jenkins laughed and shook her head.

Tish leaned forward. "I want every single detail, do you hear me?" She flopped back in her chair and sighed. "Was he wonderful?"

"I don't know!"

"What?"

"I told you, I don't remember anything that happened last night after Douglas was called away. I don't have any idea how I ended up in Ross Tracy's bed. All I know is that when I woke up this morning with the mother of all hangovers, I was wearing a man's pajama top and nothing else, and Ross Tracy was lying in the same bed less than six inches away. Thank God I managed to slip out without waking him." She groaned. "Tish, it was a nightmare."

Tish snorted. "I wouldn't exactly call *that* a nightmare. A dream come true maybe, but certainly not a nightmare."

"Tish, be serious."

"I'm as serious as a heart attack."

"Oh God, Tish, what if we . . . you know . . . did something."

Tish shrugged. "What if you did?"

"I don't know if he used protection."

Tish looked confused. "Are you worried that he made you pregnant?"

Jenkins rolled her eyes. "Don't be silly, of course not." Then she looked thoughtful. "Although that's not an impossibility, either, come to think of it. But I'm more worried about disease—like AIDS, for instance."

Both Tish's brows rose. "I hadn't thought of that."

"Yeah? Well, I've thought of little else."

Tish slumped back. "All right," she said, her tone matter-of-fact. "It appears that there's only one thing you can do."

"And what, pray tell, is that?"

"You have to ask him, of course."

Jenkins sputtered and then stared, incredulous, at Tish. "Have you completely lost your mind? You expect me just to call him up and say, 'Excuse me, Detective Tracy, but did we have sex last night? And if we did, did we use protection?' "

"Don't say 'did we have sex.' " Tish interjected. "Say, 'did we make love.' It sounds better."

Jenkins rolled her eyes and put her head in her hands. "You're no help at all, Tish," she said. "And, now, if you'll excuse me, I think I'm going to be sick."

Six

Saturday morning Jenkins put a load of laundry in the washing machine and then sighed. It had been three days since her birthday and she was still feeling the effects of her champagne hangover. After turning on the washing machine, she decided to pamper herself. Today was a good day for a facial and an oil treatment for her hair.

Jenkins slathered her hair with mayonnaise and then wrapped her head in plastic wrap. She'd discovered that though the mayonnaise made her smell like a sandwich, it left her hair more healthy-looking than expensive salon treatments.

She topped the plastic wrap with a hot towel and, while the mayonnaise and heat were doing their magic, she smoothed a commercial mud pack on her face. Then, with the rhythmic whump-whump of the washing machine in the background, she stretched out on the family room floor, propped her feet on a hassock, and closed her eyes. She'd been dozing when the doorbell rang.

"Must be Tish," she murmured as she pushed herself up from the floor. She'd nearly forgotten that Tish had volunteered to pick up donated clothing for the local domestic violence shelter.

Jenkins retrieved the large plastic bag of clothes from the hall closet, shuffled sleepily to the front door, and threw it open.

"Hi, Tish, I—" She stopped mid-sentence and the bag of clothes dropped from her suddenly nerveless fingers.

"Hi."

Mayonnaise oozed down her mud-covered brow as Jenkins stared, speechless, at Ross Tracy. How was it possible for a man to look this good dressed in jeans and a bomber jacket?

"Guess I should have called first," he said, a devastating grin creasing his face. "Do you want me to come back later?"

"N-no, of course not." Jenkins murmured. He'd

already seen her, she thought gloomily. She would have frowned, but she didn't want to crack the dried mud on her face. She opened the door wider.

"You've got a nice place," Ross said, looking around.

"Thanks," Jenkins mumbled and gestured for him to go on into the family room. Pointing to herself, she said, "Be right back."

"I need to check in at the station. May I use your phone?"

She nodded and pointed to the phone on the table by the sofa. She hoped he talked a long time, at least long enough for her to make herself presentable.

Ross smiled when Jenkins returned to the room. For some reason he always felt like smiling when he saw her. She looked like a teenager this morning. Her hair was still damp and piled on top of her head. She'd washed the gunk off her face and had changed out of the baggy sweats into a pair of jeans and a sweater. And, he noticed, she was barefoot.

"Well, now," she said, looking uneasy. "To what do I owe this visit? Something to do with the robbery?"

Ross shook his head. "I wanted to return your property."

"You mean you've found my missing wallet? I was sure I'd never see that again, and—" She paused when Ross shook his head again. "You didn't find my wallet?"

Smiling, Ross reached under his jacket to the back

pocket of his jeans. "Thought you might be needing this."

Looped over his finger was the bronze sandal she'd left at his apartment. He watched the skin beneath her freckles turn crimson. "I found it just outside the back door," he continued. "It must have fallen off when I carried you from the car."

Jenkins eased down to the large leather hassock. "Ah. Well, I've been wanting to talk with you about that."

Ross nodded. "I sort of figured you might." He sat across from her and waited for her to speak.

Jenkins swallowed and licked her lips. "I don't remember much about that night."

His grin broadened. "No, I somehow didn't think you would."

"How did I come to be with you?"

"I spotted you leaving the restaurant. You weren't in any shape to drive, so I offered to drive you home."

"But you didn't—drive me home, I mean."

He smiled wryly. "I couldn't. I didn't know where you lived and I couldn't get you to tell me."

"I refused to tell you my address?"

Ross laughed. "No, you passed out cold the moment I put you in the car. I looked in your purse hoping to find something with an address on it, but no luck." He arched a brow. "You really shouldn't go out without a driver's license, Jinx."

"I know. My license is in my missing wallet and I haven't gotten around to getting a duplicate." She chewed her lip a moment. "So, since you didn't know my address, you took me home with you?"

"That's about the size of it."

"Do you usually do that?"

He barked a laugh. "Hardly."

"Then why did you?"

That's a good question, Ross thought. Why had he taken her home when he could have called the station for a license check that would have given her address?

"Ross?"

He blinked and shrugged. "I was tired, it had been a long day and I found you just at the end of my shift. I figured I'd take you home to sleep it off and I'd get some rest." He chuckled. "However, it was a while before I got any rest."

Jenkins swallowed. "What do you mean?"

"I mean," he said, grinning at the memory of all that had happened that night. "You kept me busy for some time."

Jenkins gasped and closed her eyes. "You mean I . . . I just can't believe I actually . . . oh, God, this is awful!"

Ross arched a brow at her outburst. "It's nothing to get so upset about. So long as you don't make a habit of it—"

"Make a habit of it!" she snapped, her tone indignant as she glowered at him. "Just what kind of woman do you think I am? Make a habit of it! Do you think I do that sort of thing all the time?"

"Well, no, but heck, you're not the first woman to—"

"I'm sure I'm not," she interrupted. "But if I hadn't drunk too much champagne I would have never even considered doing . . . it!" She stood up and began pacing the room. "Despite my actions to the contrary, Detective Tracy, I am not that kind of girl . . . er . . . woman."

Ross was taken aback at her vehement response. What was the big deal? Lots of women—men, too, for that matter—had a little too much to drink on occasion. And while it might be embarrassing for them, it certainly didn't warrant this kind of reaction.

"Jinx, I don't—"

She whirled to face him. "I just have one question for you, Detective Tracy, and I'd appreciate an honest answer."

He shrugged, "Okay, ask away."

She drew in a deep breath and let it out slowly. "When you and I . . . did . . . it. Did you. . . ." She covered her face with her hands. "I can't believe I have to ask you this."

Ross frowned. "What? Did I what?"

Hands over her face, she mumbled, "Didyouuseprotection?"

He blinked, confused. "What?"

She took her hands from her face and, avoiding his eyes, whispered, "I need to know if you used protection."

Ross stared for a moment as her question sunk in. He grinned. Then he chuckled. Finally, he threw back his head and laughed long and hard.

She glared at him. "This isn't funny, damn you!"

He was laughing so hard he could hardly speak. "Oh, yes ma'am, it is! Now I get it! Ha ha . . . oh, Jinx . . . hee hee . . . you actually thought that we . . . ha ha ha ha—ow!" He cupped his cheek and fell back in the chair. "Why'd you slap me?"

Standing over him with her arms crossed, she said,

"In the movies, somebody always slaps the hysterical person."

"Damn it, I wasn't hysterical and this isn't the movies."

Jenkins struck an exaggerated Betty Boop pose, laid her finger against her cheek and fluttered her lashes. "Oops," she said in a voice that lacked a modicum of sincerity. "My mistake."

Ross rubbed his burning cheek and wondered if it bore a red imprint of her palm. "Damn, that hurt," he grumbled.

"Serves you right for laughing at me." She slumped back on the hassock. "Am I to infer from your less-than-flattering reaction that nothing untoward happened between us?"

He smiled crookedly. "Nothing happened. We spent the night in the same bed, but all we did was sleep."

"Then why was I dressed—and I use the term loosely—in nothing but a smile and your pajama top?"

"Because you sold Buicks on your clothes."

"I did what?"

"Sold Buicks, called for Ralph, tossed your cookies, blew hash—in other words, you threw up. After helping you shower, I put you in my pajama top and tucked you into bed—where you slept, unmolested, for the rest of the night."

"You undressed me?" she squeaked.

"Did you expect me to put you in my bed with vomit on your clothes? Sorry, but I wasn't about to do that."

"But that means you saw me—"

He grinned wickedly. "Naked as the day you were born."

She grabbed a pillow off the sofa and began hitting him with it. "I can't believe you did that, Ross Tracy!"

He started laughing again and could hardly fend off the cushioned blows. "Stop!" he yelled, "Uncle! Uncle!"

She sat back down and pressed her face into the pillow. She mumbled something, but Ross couldn't understand what she said. He reached up and tried to pull the pillow away. "Hey, don't be upset. I didn't really look at you. It was all very clinical, I swear it." Yeah, he thought wryly, and if you believe that, sweetheart, I've got some swamp land for sale.

She sighed then and looked at her hands. "I suppose I should thank you for taking care of me. Not many people would have bothered taking care of an inebriated woman—especially one who'd—what did you call it? One who'd . . . sold Buicks? I appreciate your looking out for me."

"My pleasure, anytime." He looked at her feet for a moment and then, taking a deep breath he said, "Jinx, would you go to dinner with me?"

She was obviously surprised. "Do you mean, like a date?"

He laughed. "Of course."

"What about your girlfriend, What's-Her-Name? The one who called you on the vibrator—I mean pager."

"Gilly. We aren't seeing each other anymore."

"Oh, I'm sorry."

He shrugged. "Don't be, I'm not." He rubbed his hands together. "So, will you go out with me?"

Still holding onto the pillow, she hugged it to her chest. "Ross, do you know how old I am?"

He grinned. "Yeah, you're forty, the big Four-Oh, as you put it. You told me the other night. Several times as I remember."

"And you still want to go out with me?"

Ross leaned forward and rested his elbows on his knees. "Jinx, why else would I have asked you?"

Jenkins studied him for a moment. "I don't know, and that's what concerns me. I'm four years older than you, I'm not rich, and I'm certainly no beauty. So why did you ask me?"

Ross was trying to think of a reply when the phone rang and Jenkins hurried to answer it. He was glad for the interruption because he wasn't sure how to answer. The truth was, he didn't know why. Why was this middle-aged woman with the unusual name the last thing he thought about when he went to sleep and the first thing on his mind when he awoke? Maybe his obsession with Jenkins McGraw was due to the life-threatening experience they'd shared that night in the grocery store. He didn't know, all he knew was that he had an almost overwhelming desire to see her, to talk with her, to be near her.

Jenkins returned to the family room. "Sorry for the interruption," she said, as she sat down. "Now, where were we?"

"You were about to agree to go out with me," Ross said. "I like you, Jinx. You're smart, you're funny, and I want to get to know you better."

She sighed. "I'm sorry, but I can't. I appreciate

the invitation, really I do, but I'm not ready to get back in the social scene."

"Look, if it'll make you feel better we won't call it a date. It'll just be two friends going out to dinner."

She shook her head. "No. I just can't."

"All right, I won't push." Ross stood up. "If you ever change your mind, you'll let me know?"

"Sure," she replied, but something in her voice told him she was lying. She stood up and walked to the door with him. "Thanks for bringing my shoe."

He reached out and cupped her cheek. "I was happy for the excuse to see you again," he murmured. Suddenly the front door opened and Ross was shoved against Jenkins.

"Oh! Sorry," the teenaged boy said as he stepped inside. He frowned suspiciously at Ross.

"Jason," Jenkins said breathlessly. "I wasn't expecting you home today."

"Jimmy had a doctor's appointment, so I rode with him."

"Ross, this is my son, Jason. Jason is a freshman at Southern Military Institute."

Ross grinned and offered his hand. "Good to meet you, Jason. I understand SMI is a pretty good school."

"Yeah, it's okay. I'd rather be here, but my dad wanted me to go to SMI like he did." Then, as if what his mother had said finally registered, Jason, obviously impressed, said, "You're a detective?"

"That's right," Ross replied.

"What division?"

"Narcotics,"

"Cool," Jason said. "I'm taking some criminal justice classes at SMI and I've got to write a paper on the search and seizure laws. I'd like to talk with you about it sometime."

Ross nodded. "Sure, just call the station and I'll be glad to talk with you." He looked back at Jenkins. "I'd better go."

She nodded. "Thanks again, for . . . everything."

When Ross was gone, Jason looked at his mother worriedly. "Why was he here?"

"He just dropped by to talk with me about the robbery."

"Oh, is that all." The obvious relief on his face was painful to see.

Jenkins ruffled his hair. "Yes, my darling son, that's all." How long, she wondered, would Jason cling to the impossible dream that one day his parents would reconcile? She'd tried talking to him about it, she'd even had him visit a psychologist in the hope that a professional could make Jason understand the way things were. But nothing had worked. He still stubbornly refused to believe that his parents' marriage was over.

Jenkins hadn't realized how bad things were until a few months ago when Tish had asked her to be a fourth for a game of bridge with one of Buzzy's colleagues. When she'd told Jason of her plans, he'd become so upset that she'd finally called and canceled. She hadn't attempted anything like that again. She couldn't bear to see her child upset and if keeping Jason happy meant she would have to do without male companionship, then so be it. After all, Jason was the most impor-

tant person in her life. She rubbed the back of
her neck and sighed. Now, if she could just stop
daydreaming about a certain detective. . . .

Seven

Jenkins painstakingly affixed the hooked rubber
nose over her own and held it there until the glue
took hold. Than she turned her head from side to
side to study the effect of the greenish-gray makeup
and the false nose. Not bad, she thought. Once I
put on the wig, I'll look exactly like an old hag.

She'd already placed a thick pad of cotton batting
on her back to produce a decided hump. After donning the wig, she had only to blacken a few of her
teeth and her costume for the Halloween party would
be complete. She giggled and then cleared her throat.
"Witches do not giggle," she admonished her reflection. "Witches cackle."

Jenkins carefully pulled the long, gray wig over
her head, tucked in a few stray red hairs, and
grinned at the stranger in the mirror. Her own
mother wouldn't recognize her in this getup. She
would be completely anonymous.

She hadn't wanted to go to Tish and Buzzy's costume party, but Tish, never one to take no for an
answer, had badgered her into accepting the invitation.

"It'll be fun," Tish had insisted. "Jason will be
out with his friends and you should be out with
yours."

So she'd agreed to go, and once she'd made the commitment, Jenkins found she was looking forward to the party.

Ready at last, Jenkins stood in front of her full-length mirror to admire her handiwork. She winked and a hunchbacked old crone winked back at her. Satisfied with her appearance, Jenkins went to the kitchen and programmed her phone to forward any calls to the Armstrong residence.

Just before leaving, she retrieved her broom from a small closet. "Can't go without transportation," she murmured with a grin. Then she headed across the backyard to Tish's house.

A glittering fairy dressed in frothy pink organdy welcomed Jenkins to the party. "Who are you?" Tish-the-Fairy asked, studying Jenkins's gray-green face.

"Just call me Hazel." Jenkins disguised her voice.

"Either I've never seen you before in my life or your costume's incredible," Tish said, her tone uncertain.

"My costume's incredible," Jenkins replied in her own voice.

Tish gasped. "Jenkins? My God, it *is* you! I can't believe it." She turned around and waved to a rotund Henry VIII. "Buzzy! Come and see Jenkins! Look everybody, it's Jenkins!"

"So much for maintaining anonymity," Jenkins muttered as Tish pulled her into the room full of people.

Jenkins knew the majority of the guests, having met them at other parties. Most were colleagues of Buzzy's and the others were Tish's eclectic selection of friends: her hairdresser, her pottery teacher, her gynecologist, her yard man, her palmist, and the waitress from her favorite coffee shop, to name a few. Tish collected friends the way some people collected stamps; and one could be sure of an interesting mix of people at her parties.

Jenkins was talking to Count Dracula about the best time of year to plant dogwood trees when Tish appeared at her side. "Jenkins, you have a phone call," she said. And when Jenkins followed her to the phone, Tish whispered, "It's the police."

Jenkins swallowed nervously as she picked up the phone. "Hello? This is Jenkins McGraw."

"Ms. McGraw, this is Sergeant Haines. I hate to call you like this, but we have a young man here who says he's your son."

"Jason?" Jenkins asked, her heart in her throat.

"Yes, ma'am. I'm afraid he's gotten into a bit of trouble."

"Oh? What kind of trouble, Sergeant?"

"He and his friends were caught throwing eggs at cars. It wasn't meant to be more than a prank, but it caused an accident."

"Oh, my God! Was anyone hurt?"

"The driver got a bump on his head, but it's not serious. Still, we'd like you to come down to the station, ma'am."

"Of course, I'll be right there. Thank you for calling, Sergeant." Jenkins's hand was shaking when she hung up the phone. Then gathering her composure, she went to find Tish.

"I'll drive you to the station," Tish said after Jenkins told her what had happened.

"You can't leave your party, Tish, you have guests."

"Buzzy can take care of the guests. What kind of

friend would I be to let you go down there by yourself? Wait here while I get my keys and apprise Buzzy
of the situation."

A moment later Tish led Jenkins out the back
door. "We'll have to take the Bug," she said, nodding toward the small car. "My Beemer's in the shop
getting new shoes."

"We could take my car," Jenkins said, eyeing the
yellow Volkswagon convertible.

"Waste of time," Tish replied. "Get in."

Jenkins folded her long frame into the tiny car
and barely managed to pull the door closed before
Tish peeled out of the driveway. "I'd like to get there
in one piece," she mumbled, grabbing the dash as
the Bug careened around the corner.

If the situation hadn't been so serious, Jenkins
would have laughed at the stunned looks they got
as they drove through the streets of Birmingham.
What a picture we must make, she thought, a pink
fairy driving and a green-gray hag riding shotgun.

Tish pulled up in front of the brick building that
housed the police department. Jumping from the
car, they hurried up the steps and pushed through
the glass doors at the entrance.

"I'm looking for Sergeant Haines," Jenkins said
to the first uniformed policeman she saw.

"Hope you didn't double-park your broom," he
said. "I'd hate to have to give you a ticket."

Confused, Jinx stared at the officer. Then she
comprehended the reason for his comment. She
had forgotten for a moment that she was in costume.
"Officer, please, I must find him."

"Didn't know he was married," the policeman

said, obviously under the impression that this was part of an elaborate joke.

Then Tish took matters in hand.

"Listen, you," Tish said, smacking the officer's shoulder with her wand. "We didn't come here to entertain the troops, understand? We have business here. Now, point us in the direction of Sergeant Haines before I turn you into a eunuch!"

The officer swallowed heavily and pointed over his shoulder. "Down the hall, around the corner, second door from the end."

Jenkins hurried in the direction he'd indicated. At the second door from the end, Jenkins didn't hesitate, but burst inside. "Sergeant Haines?" she said breathlessly. "I'm Jenkins McGraw and I'm here about my son, Jason."

The man behind the desk stared and after a moment's hesitation said, "Sergeant Haines is talking to some other parents, ma'am. Have a seat in the hall and he'll be with you shortly."

"Is my son all right? May I see him?" she asked.

"He's fine. He's with a juvenile officer right now."

"Shouldn't he have a lawyer with him?" Tish asked, coming to stand beside Jenkins.

The officer's eyes widened slightly when he saw the pink fairy, but he recovered quickly. "He's got a lawyer with him, ma'am. His daddy sent one."

"Is Jake here?" Jenkins asked.

"No, ma'am. He just sent a lawyer." The officer nodded toward the door. "If you . . . ladies will just wait outside?"

Jenkins left the office and sat down on the hard bench. "Damn Jake," she said, rubbing her temples.

"What kind of father would send an attorney instead of coming down himself?"

Tish patted her shoulder. "At least Jason will know he's got one parent who cares about him."

"I know, but it's Jake that Jason wants, not me. I wouldn't be surprised if this whole thing tonight wasn't done to get Jake's attention." Jenkins bit her lip. "He must be so scared."

"He'll be all right."

"I wish they'd let me see him." Close to tears, Jenkins envisioned her son sitting beneath a single lightbulb while two gravelly voiced, chain-smoking cops interrogated him.

Ross Tracy climbed out of the red sports car. "Go on home and get some rest, Kelly," he said to his partner. "I'll take care of the paperwork on this case."

"Thanks, Ross. I'll owe you one."

"Damn straight you will," Ross said with a grin. "Just take care of that cold. I don't want you laid up with the flu."

Ross watched his friend drive away before trudging up the steps of the station house. He stopped to speak to the dispatcher and then headed down the hall. He turned a corner and stopped at the office he shared with Kelly. As he was removing his key, he spied the witch and fairy seated in the hall.

Ross grinned to himself as he unlocked the door. Never a dull moment around here, he thought as he started inside. But he caught a whiff of a familiar fragrance and he paused on the threshold. Turning slowly, he walked toward the two costumed women. "Jinx?" he said hesitantly. "Is that you?"

The hideous witch turned toward him, stood up, and promptly burst into tears. "Oh, Ross, I'm so glad to see you."

"Hey," he soothed, gathering her into his arms. "What's wrong?"

"It's Jason," she sobbed. "He's been arrested." Then Jenkins pushed out of his arms. "I'm sorry," she said, sniffing. "I'm usually not the hysterical type. I've just been so worried about Jason and we've been waiting such a long time to see him." She looked back at Tish. "Do you have a tissue? My nose is running."

"A nose like that doesn't run, Jenkins, it gallops," Tish quipped as she handed her friend a tissue.

Ross covered his mouth to hide his grin. It was all he could do not to laugh out loud. God, what a costume. He could hardly bear to look at her.

Steeling himself, Ross focused on the one familiar thing about her: her eyes, her dream-haunting, golden eyes. "What sort of trouble?" he asked, and then, "Never mind, I'll find out. You just wait here until I do."

"Will you see if he's okay, please?"

"Just relax, Jinx. Everything's going to be all right."

Jenkins watched Ross move purposely down the hall and felt some of the tension leave her. Everything is going to be all right, she thought. She didn't know why the knowledge that Ross was seeing to things should make any difference, but it did. Ross

Tracy was a hero as far as she was concerned. He was her knight in shining armor, and she was his. . . .

"Oh, God!"

"What's wrong?" a startled Tish asked.

"What's wrong? Look at me, Tish! I'm a hag!"

Tish blinked. "Yes, you are. So?"

"I just threw myself, blubbering, into Ross Tracy's arms like some hysterical damsel in distress, and just look at me!"

Tish giggled. "So you're a hysterical old crone in distress. So what? It didn't seem to bother him."

Jenkins slumped against the wall. "Why couldn't I have chosen a pretty costume—something like a princess or a harem girl? Even a lady vampire oozes sexuality. But I chose to be a hunchbacked crone so ugly I'd snag lightning. It's humiliating."

Tish patted her shoulder. "Nobody ever died of humiliation. You'll get over it."

Jenkins sighed morosely. "Yeah, I guess so." She looked at her watch. "Honey, you've been here with me for over an hour. You need to get back to your party. We'll take a cab home."

"I wouldn't dream of making you take a cab. I brought you, I'll wait until you can leave."

"But you have guests."

"Forget the guests."

"I'll take her home, Tish." Both women turned to see Ross walking toward them. "Jason will be out in about five minutes," he said." Jinx, you'll need to fill out some forms, and then you and Jason can go home."

"Thank God," Jenkins sighed.

"Great news," Tish said. Then she stood up.

"Since I know you'll be in good hands, I'll get back to my party."

Jenkins hugged her friend. "Thank you so much, Tish. You're always there when I need you."

"I'll call you tomorrow, okay?"

Jenkins nodded, afraid to speak lest she start crying again. She was staring at her hands when Ross knelt at her knee. "Jason's fine, Jinx, and he hasn't been arrested. He and his friends just played a prank that backfired."

"Sergeant Haines said they caused someone to have an accident and ruined the man's car."

"That's true, but even the victim knows it wasn't intentional. And the car has a smashed fender, it's not totaled. I expect five or six hundred dollars will take care of the repair. Divide that between ten kids and it's not going to amount to all that much in restitution."

"Mom?"

Jenkins stood up and held out her arms to her son. "Jason, are you all right?"

The boy, obviously tired and scared, hung his head. "We didn't mean to hurt anybody, mom."

Jenkins hugged him. "I know you didn't. We'll talk about it tomorrow, honey, after we've both had a good night's sleep."

Sergeant Haines stepped into the hallway. "If you'll just sign these papers, Mrs. McGraw, you can take Jason home."

Jenkins took the papers, scribbled her name several times, and then handed them back to him. "That's some costume, Mrs. McGraw," the sergeant said, grinning.

Jenkins blushed beneath her greenish-gray makeup. "I know I must look a sight. I was at a Halloween party when you called."

Haines chuckled. "I kind of figured that."

"Let's go, you two," Ross said. He put his arms around Jenkins's and Jason's shoulders and led them out of the building.

Eight

They didn't talk much on the trip home. Jason, Jenkins noticed, was unusually quiet—not surprising, she supposed, considering tonight had been his first and, she fervently hoped, his last brush with the law. She was trying to think of a way to cheer him up as Ross slowed to a stop in front of her house.

"You know," she said suddenly, "I'm in the mood for some hot cocoa. How does that sound to you, kid?"

Jason didn't reply and Jenkins turned to look in the back seat at him. "Would you like some cocoa?"

Jason shrugged. "I guess."

"How about you, Detective Tracy? Would you like to join Jason and me for some cocoa?"

"Sounds good, if you're sure you want to go to the trouble?"

"I'm positive. It will make us all feel better."

They entered the house from the garage and walked directly into the kitchen. Jenkins flipped on the lights and motioned for Ross to take a seat at the breakfast table. Ross pulled off his jacket and hung it over his chair. Then Jenkins busied herself making the cocoa, measuring the simple ingredients and pouring milk into a pan. Jason seemed to ignore both Ross and his mother as he headed down the hall toward his room.

Jenkins paused before she mixed the sugar into the dark brown powder. "Jay, where are you going?"

Jason stopped and looked back at her. "I'm going to call Kathy."

"Honey, it's nearly midnight. I don't think you should call her at this hour."

Jason put his hands on his hips. "Look, mom, I told her I'd call as soon as I got home. She's expecting to hear from me tonight, so I'm going to call her."

Jenkins flashed a quick glance at Ross and then sighed heavily. "All right, go ahead and call her. But if her parents get angry. . . ."

"I know, don't say you didn't warn me." He started out of the room and then paused in the doorway. "I'm going to bed after I talk with Kathy. I'm not really in the mood for hot cocoa anymore."

"That's fine with me. Detective Tracy and I will have our cocoa without you," she said, trying to hide the fact that she was embarrassed by Jason's sudden surliness. When Jason started to leave again, Jenkins called to him.

"What now?" Jason snapped.

Jenkins gave him her best watch-your-mouth-young-man glare. "Isn't there something you want to say to Detective Tracy?"

He seemed at first not to understand what she was talking about. Then he sighed and said, "Oh, yeah. Thanks for giving my mom and me a ride home, Detective Tracy."

"Glad to be of service, Jason."

Jason looked at Jenkins as if to say, May I go now?

"You may go make your call, Jason, but don't stay on the phone too long." Jenkins said firmly.

He muttered something under his breath as he strode out of the room.

"I apologize for my son's behavior," Jenkins murmured as she watched Jason disappear down the hall. "He hasn't been himself since Jake and I divorced."

"Divorce is tough on kids," Ross acknowledged.

"Yes, it is. But I want you to know he isn't always like this. Most of the time Jason is a pretty nice kid. But when he's upset or disappointed he becomes a bit antagonistic. I've talked with a therapist and his guidance counselor about the best way to handle these situations, but no one's been able to give me any practical answers. So I just deal with it as best I can."

Jenkins poured the steaming cocoa into mugs and brought them to the table. "I also want to apologize for my own behavior this evening." She sat down across from him. "Believe it or not, I am not the teeth-gnashing, hair-tearing, hysterical type."

Ross grinned. "Don't apologize. You were upset. You're a mother, after all, and mothers sometimes get overwrought when their kids are in trouble."

"I know, but I pride myself on being able to handle almost any situation."

"I think you handled the situation well, considering what had happened." He sipped from his mug. "Good cocoa."

"Would you like a cookie or something to go with it, Ross? I think there are some marshmallows in the pantry."

"This is fine, really." Ross leaned forward. "Jinx, why do you call me Detective Tracy when Jason's around, and Ross when he isn't?"

She looked down at her cocoa. "I-I don't want Jason to think there's anything going on between us," she finally said.

"That should be fairly easy," Ross said. "Because, unless I've missed something, there isn't a damned thing going on between us. At least, not yet."

She shook her head. "And there can't be."

"Because of Jason?"

Jenkins nodded. "Jason gets really upset if I even consider going out with anyone. He still believes that his father and I will reconcile someday, though I've told him over and over that it'll never happen."

"And you're fostering his mistaken belief when you don't go out. It seems to me that the kindest thing to do would be to get on with your life. Eventually, Jason has to accept the truth."

Jenkins leaned back in her chair and sighed. "You may be right, but he's been hurt so much and I'm the one person he can count on not to abandon him. Jake never had much time for Jason while we were married, and now that we're divorced, he has even less time for him. I don't want Jason to feel he has to compete for my attention the way he does for his father's. At least not right now."

Ross frowned. "You're afraid if you and I see each other socially, Jason will see me as someone who'd usurp his place with you. In other words, I'd be a threat."

"Exactly."

Ross finished his cocoa. "Well," he said as he carefully set down his mug. "At least I've learned one good thing tonight."

"And what is that?"

"That your refusing to go out with me doesn't necessarily mean you don't like me."

She avoided his gaze. "Oh, no. Quite the contrary, Ross. I'm afraid I like you entirely too much."

Ross stood up. "I guess I'd better be going. Thanks for the cocoa."

Jenkins walked him to the door and switched on the outside light. She looked at the floor and murmured, "Thank you again for what you did tonight. Your being there made the incident much less frightening for both Jason and me." When he didn't say anything, she looked up at him and found he was studying her.

"What's wrong? Why are you looking at me like that?"

He grinned. "I was just thinking that this is the first time I've ever had an overwhelming urge to kiss a hag."

Jenkins gasped. "Oh, my stars! I forgot I still had on this horrid makeup! Why didn't you say something?"

Ross shrugged. "Actually, I've gotten sort of used to it. However, I haven't figured out how to kiss you without being impaled on that wicked looking nose." He pulled her into his arms. "Nevertheless," he said, "I would certainly like to see if it can be done."

"Ross, I—"

"Shhhh," he admonished. "This is going to take some serious contemplation."

Her heart pounding, Jenkins held her breath as Ross tilted his head this way and that, searching for a way to kiss her. Finally, his lips found hers and his arms drew her more firmly into his embrace.

Maybe it was because it had been so long since she'd been kissed the way a woman ought to be kissed, or maybe it was simply the fact that it was Ross who was kissing her, but for whatever reason, Jenkins felt every nerve in her body come alive the moment his lips closed over hers. Her senses heightened, her fingertips noted the weave of the fabric of his shirt; she was conscious of the soft cotton beneath her costume sliding against her skin as Ross's hands roved over her back; she was aware of Ross's subtle, musky scent mingling with her perfume to form a new, intoxicating fragrance, and she savored the rich, dark taste of chocolate when his sleek tongue delved deeper in her mouth.

And when he broke the kiss, Jenkins felt strangely bereft.

Ross pressed his brow against hers. "I never knew crones could taste so good," he said.

She laughed softly. "I never knew cops tasted like chocolate, either."

He sighed, and rested his chin on the top of her head. "I don't know how, but I'm going to figure out a way for us to see each other without hurting Jason."

She backed away and shook her head. "I don't think that's possible."

He shrugged on his jacket. "Nothing's impossible, Jinx. You'll just have to trust me on that." He squeezed her hands. "I gotta go. But I'll be seeing you again, soon. And that's not a threat, Jinx, it's a promise."

Nine

The doorbell pealed through the dark house, jolting Jenkins out of a sound sleep. She sat up. Had Jason forgotten his key? Blinking away her sleepiness, she glanced over at the clock on the bedside table. The glowing green numbers said four a.m.—much too early for Jason, whose ride usually dropped him off around seven. So who was ringing her doorbell at this hour? She clutched her throat as her heart began to pound as if she'd just run a ten-mile race. What if Jason had been in an accident?

The doorbell pealed again and, as mounting dread stole her breath, Jenkins leapt out of bed. Without even taking time to pull a robe over her thin cotton T-shirt, she dashed down the hall, flipping on lights as she went. At the door, she stood on tiptoe to peer though the peephole. The sight on the other side made her gasp out loud and she tumbled with the deadbolt lock and threw open the door.

"Ross," she said, taking him by the hand and pulling him inside. "What on earth happened to you?"

He was holding a handkerchief to his head, but blood still managed to trickle down the side of his face. "I had a wreck," he said. "About a block from here."

She dragged him into the kitchen and pulled out a stool. "Get that jacket off and sit," she said. "You can tell me what happened while I have a look at your head."

Ross tossed his leather bomber jacket over the back of a chair and eased down on the stool. "I'd just gone off duty, dropped my partner Kelly off at his place, and was on my way home when some drunk ran a stop sign and rammed into me."

Jenkins carefully removed the handkerchief from the wound. "You've got quite a gash above your eye. I think it may need a stitch or two."

"Nah, it's all right. Just pull it together with a strip of adhesive and it'll be fine."

"I don't know, it looks deep."

"It'll be fine. I heal fast."

The look in his eyes told her that arguing the point would be a waste of breath, so she sighed and said, "All right, if you say so."

She went to the sink and ran some warm water into a bowl, then searched an overhead cabinet for her first aid kit. She brought the bowl of water to the kitchen table and rummaged through the first aid kit for the things she'd need to patch him up.

Ross sat with his heels propped on the rungs of the wooden stool. Even seated he was so tall that Jenkins had to stand between his knees to get close enough to reach the injury above his eye.

"Let me clean this a little bit and then I'll see what I can do about bandaging it." She dabbed at the gash with a moist square of gauze and Ross flinched. "I'm sorry," she murmured.

"S'okay."

After cleaning off the dried blood, Jenkins moistened another square of gauze with rubbing alcohol. "Maybe this will kill any germs still lingering in there," she mumbled, squeezing the gauze so that the alcohol dripped inside the wound.

Ross jerked back. "Holy cow!" he yelped. "That burns like a son of a bitch!"

"I'm sorry," she said, stifling a giggle. "Hold still and I'll blow on it until it stops stinging."

He grimaced, but he sat still. Jenkins rested her hands on his shoulders as she stood on tiptoe and blew softly on the torn flesh. After a moment she asked, "Better?"

"Yeah," he replied in a somewhat husky voice. "Sorry to put you to so much trouble."

"That's all right," she said, carefully applying a strip of adhesive tape to the cut and then covering the whole thing with clean gauze. "How is it you happened to be so close to my house? If you were going home from Kelly's, weren't you a good distance out of your way? I thought you told me Kelly lived on the south side of town."

"He does. But I always drive by here before I go home."

She paused and looked down at him. This was a surprise to her. She hadn't seen or heard from him since Halloween night—and that had been over a week ago.

"You do? Whatever for?"

He shrugged. "Just to see that you're okay. The fact that we still haven't caught Ray Price worries me. Until we get him behind bars for good, I'll sleep better knowing that you're all right."

Having finished applying the dressing to his injury, Jenkins sank into a chair across from him. "Why, Ross, I had no idea you were watching my house." She patted his blue-jeaned knee. "Thank you for that."

He grinned and pointed to his bandaged brow. "Thank you for this," he replied.

She looked at the bandage and frowned. "Oh, darn, one of the strips of tape is coming loose. Hold still while I replace it with another one." She stood between his knees again and retaped the loosened bandage. "There," she said, "that should hold it."

She started to back away when Ross's hands settled on her hips. "Don't move," he said.

Her breath caught. "Why? What's wrong?"

He looked at her and grinned. "Nothing's wrong, I just like having you within reach." He pulled her closer, so that her breasts just barely grazed his chest and she inhaled sharply at the contact. She put her hands on his shoulders, intending to push him away, but something in his eyes prevented her from doing it. Uncertain, she moistened her dry lips.

"Jinx, I just want to hold you," he said softly. His large hands caressed her back and it suddenly occurred to her that she was practically naked, wearing nothing but one of Jason's old T-shirts and what she called her granny panties. The fact that she could actually feel the rough calluses on Ross's fingers substantiated her fear that the ancient T-shirt was threadbare to the point of being practically nonexistent.

"I-I should put on a robe," she stammered.

"Don't," he said softly. "I like you like this." His hands continued to stroke her, soothing, calming her, while his deep, husky voice lulled her into complacency.

"I must say, Mrs. McGraw," Ross teased. "You are a great deal lovelier tonight than when last I saw you." He leaned forward and nuzzled her neck as his forearm settled around her hips to draw them more snugly into the cradle of his thighs.

Jenkins closed her eyes and gave a shuddering sigh as his lips planted light kisses up her neck and then moved to nibble her earlobe. And when his tongue traced the shape of her ear, shivers of desire raced through her veins. She turned her face toward his, seeking, until at last his mouth closed over hers, gently devouring. Her hands slid around his neck as she gave over to the passion his gentle seduction had ignited.

Raising his mouth from hers, Ross gazed into her eyes. "Jinx," he murmured, "I want to touch you."

"What?"

His gaze drifted from her eyes to settle on her breasts and she understood what he was asking. And though her body ached for his touch, Jenkins couldn't quite bring herself to say the words he wanted to hear. She could only look at him and hope that he could read permission in her eyes. He hold her gaze for a long moment and then his hands slowly swept over the soft fabric of the T-shirt to fondle her swollen, peaked breasts. Her rock hard nipples thrust against the thin fabric of the shirt as if begging to be caressed. Ross smiled and then dipped his head to take one of the aching peaks into his mouth. The moment she felt the moist heat, Jenkins gasped and her hands involuntarily clenched and unclenched like cats' paws on his massive shoulders.

When the front of the T-shirt was damp from his lips and tongue, Ross rose to kiss her again. His mouth moved across her cheek and jaw to her ear, and he whispered, "I want to see you."

This time there was no doubt as to his meaning and Jenkins avoided his gaze as she slowly nodded her acquiescence.

Gently, Ross set her away from him and slowly raised the hem of the T-shirt until her breasts were revealed. "Ah, Jinx," he whispered, almost reverently, "You're beautiful." He tugged the shirt the rest of the way off and tossed it aside. Then he cupped her breasts in his hands and bent to worship them once more with his lips and tongue. Jenkins moaned and grasped his head between her hands.

Suddenly, Ross sat up, skinned off his T-shirt and, as if he couldn't wait to feel her softness against him, he pulled her to him almost roughly, crushing her to his chest. Jenkins reveled in the feel of hard muscles pressing against her aching, throbbing breasts, and she was aware of his heart thudding against her own. His hands roved over her body, exploring every inch of her, moving ever lower until one hand slipped past the elastic band of the high-waisted, serviceable panties, and searched out the core of her desire. When he touched that most intimate part of her, her breath caught and she tensed. She opened her mouth to protest, but his lips stopped the words before they could even be formed. And while his fingers parted her to slide within the sleek wetness, his tongue delved into her mouth to mimic the rhythm of his stroking fingers. Fully aroused now, her breath coming in gasps, Jenkins instinctively arched against his hand as each stroke sent jolts of pleasure through her.

Ross's breathing was labored. Taking her hand, he guided it to the thick ridge between his legs. His voice was husky, his breath hot against her ear when he spoke again. "Jinx," he breathed, "I want to make love to you."

Trembling, she clung to him. Stirred by the awakening of long-dormant desire, she felt like a breathless girl of eighteen again. His gaze traveled over her face and searched her eyes, questioning. "Yes," she finally managed, "please."

"Where?"

The words seemed not to want to leave her throat. "My . . . my bedroom . . . at the end of the hall."

Ross swung her into his arms as if she weighed nothing and strode purposely down the hall. In her bedroom, he eased her onto the rumpled bed, skinned off his jeans, and sat down on the edge of the mattress.

"You're sure?" he asked, pushing a tendril of hair from her eyes. "You don't have to do this, you know."

She searched his face. "H-have you changed your mind?"

He laughed softly, huskily, and shook his head. "God, no! I just want to be sure you want this as much as I do."

"I'm sure it's what I want, Ross, but I'm nervous. It's been a long time since . . . since. . . ."

He stretched out beside her on the bed and then raised up on his elbow to gaze down at her. "How long has it been since you've made love?"

"Seven years."

She saw a flicker of incredulity in his eyes and then it was gone and replaced with a smile. "Don't worry, Jinx," he said as his hand gently stroked her ultra-sensitive skin from shoulder to thigh, "I'm a very good teacher." Then he grinned. "Besides," he said, as he began peeling off her cotton panties, "making love is like riding a bicycle—you never really forget how."

She swallowed hard, trying not to mind the fact that she was lying naked before a very large, breathtakingly handsome, very virile man. "I-I think we may have a problem."

He was sitting on the edge of the bed removing the last of his clothing. At her mumbled comment, he looked over his shoulder. "What problem?"

"I never learned to ride a bicycle."

He laughed then and stretched out beside her. He kissed her nose, her eyes, her chin.

"Forget about the bicycle, Jinx," he murmured against her lips. "I'll teach you to ride me."

And with that he rolled over, bringing her with him so that she was lying over him, flesh against flesh, man against woman. She squirmed against his arousal and his answering moan was a heady reward. "God, Jinx," he murmured, "I want—"

"Mom? I'm home!" came a distant voice.

Jenkins gasped. "Oh, no! It's Jason!" she whispered.

Ten

"Mom? You awake?" This time Jason's voice was just outside her bedroom door.

Jenkins quickly sat up. "D-don't come in! I just got out of the shower and I'm not dressed yet."

"Well, hurry up. I have something to show you."

Jenkins scrambled off the bed and snatched her

robe from inside her closet. "Jason, honey, go put on a pot of coffee," she called as she frantically belted her robe. "I seem to be moving a little slowly this morning."

"It's taken care of. I made it the moment I got home. I'll pour a cup and bring it to you."

My God, Jenkins thought, as she heard Jason's footsteps retreating down the hall. How long had he been home? He must have come in soon after Ross carried her to the bedroom. She put a hand to her chest and closed her eyes. If Jason had come in a minute or two earlier. . . .

She ran to the door and locked it, then spun to face Ross, who was still lying in bed, looking right at home.

"You've got to leave," she whispered frantically. "I can't have Jason find you here—especially not like this!"

Ross raised up on his elbow and grinned at her. "How do you propose to get me out of here without Jason seeing me?"

Jenkins chewed her lip. How could she get a six-foot-six man out of her bedroom without his being seen? "Oh, God!"

"I've got your coffee, mom. Are you decent yet?"

Jenkins snatched Ross's clothes off the floor and bundled them into a ball. "Quick," she whispered, frantically shoving the bundle at Ross. "Under the bed!"

"What?" Ross looked at her as if she'd lost her mind.

"Please, Ross, don't argue. Just do it!"

Shaking his head, he slid off the bed and squeezed

under it. "You're going to owe me for this, Jinx, big time."

"Yes, yes, I know. I'll make it up to you. Just hide!"

When she was sure Ross was hidden, she unlocked her door. "Sorry I took so long, Jason. Guess I'm not awake yet."

Jason handed her the cup of coffee and walked inside. "I'll say. That lukewarm coffee was steaming hot when I brought it." He sat down on the end of the bed. "By the way, whose bomber jacket is hanging on the chair in the kitchen?"

Jenkins nearly choked on her coffee. "B-bomber jacket?"

"Yeah, the brown leather one."

"Oh, that. Uh, that belongs to Detective Tracy."

"When was he here?"

"Last night. He came to tell me about, um, Ray Price."

"Who's Ray Price?"

"The robber—the one they haven't caught yet."

"Oh." Her son his head. "What about the T-shirts?"

"T-shirts?" she repeated, feeling awfully stupid.

"Yeah, two of them were on the floor."

Jenkins saw in her mind's eye the image of Ross peeling off first her T-shirt and then his and tossing them to the floor, and her breasts tingled with the memory of being pressed against his smooth, muscular chest.

"Earth to mom, come in?"

"What? Oh, those T-shirts were all worn out, silly," she stammered. "I used them to wipe up a spill."

"Must have been some spill," Jason muttered.

Eager to change the subject, Jenkins sat beside

Jason at the foot of the bed. "You said you had something to show me."

"Oh, yeah." Jason drew out a folded piece of newspaper from his pocket. "I found this ad for a 1985 Harley Davidson. It says it's in good condition and the price is reasonable."

Jenkins stood and began to pace as she looked at the newspaper ad. Then she faced her son. "Jason, you know how I feel about motorcycles. They're too dangerous."

"Mom, lots of guys at school ride hogs. I'll be careful. I won't do anything stupid."

"Jason, if a car hits you, it won't matter who's at fault. You'll be just as dead."

"Why is it that you have to think of the worst possible thing that could go wrong? Why can't you be like my friends' parents? It's not like I'm asking for a race car."

"I'm sorry, Jason, but as your mother I have to consider what might happen. What your friends' parents do is their business, and if they want to gamble with their children's lives by letting them ride pigs, then—"

"What? Who said anybody was riding pigs?"

"You did. You said that lots of guys ride pigs and—"

"Hogs, mom, not pigs. A Harley is called a *hog*."

"Oh." Jenkins heard a faint but distinctive male snort. She glanced down and saw Ross's laughing face peeking from beneath the dust ruffle.

"Mom? What's the matter with you?"

Jenkins's hands fluttered to her hair, her throat, and then to her robe's already knotted belt. "There's nothing wrong with me."

"Well, you look like you've just seen a ghost—

you're so pale your freckles are practically three-dimensional."

"Jason, you do have such a way with words," she said dryly.

"Sorry, but I just call 'em as I see 'em." He sighed then. "Won't you just think about the motorcycle?"

She shook her head. "No, I'm sorry. You know I'd do almost anything for you, honey, but as far as I'm concerned, I'd just as soon buy you a loaded gun as a motorcycle."

Jason bolted up from the bed. "There you go, over-dramatizing things again. Dad was right, you are stupid!"

"Jason!"

He strode toward the door. "I'm getting out of here."

"Where are you going?"

"I'm going to see dad. Maybe I can have an intelligent conversation with him!" He stormed out of the room and a minute later she heard the front door slam.

Jenkins sighed heavily. "Ross, you can come out now."

Ross eased out from under the bed and began donning his clothes. "You all right?" he asked, buttoning his blue jeans.

She nodded. "I guess you heard everything."

He swept his long hair from his face and nodded. "Yeah, I heard." He moved up beside her and put an arm around her shoulders. "Don't take it so hard, Jinx," he said, wiping away a solitary tear that clung to her lashes.

She sighed and leaned against him. "He called me stupid."

Ross drew her to him. "He didn't mean it, sweetheart, he was just frustrated because you wouldn't give him his way."

"Do you think I'm wrong for not buying him that . . . what did he call it?"

"That *pig?*" Ross supplied with a grin and she giggled in spite of her misery. He cupped her face with his hands and gazed down at her. "No, I don't think you were wrong—but not for the reason you gave him."

She was confused. "What do you mean?"

"I mean, if Jason wants a motorcycle, he should buy one."

"B-but you said—"

"I said 'he' should buy one, not have you buy it for him. I wanted a motorcycle when I was his age and I got one—as a matter of fact, I still have it. But I worked every single day until I earned enough money to pay for it."

"But Jason's in school and—"

"Hey, I was in school, too, but I managed to find work after school and on weekends." He made a wry face. "I hate to have to tell you this, Jinx, but your little boy is a spoiled brat."

She pushed out of his arms. "How dare you say that about him? You don't even know him."

"I don't have to know him. Any kid who talks to his mother the way he talked to you just now is a spoiled brat." He shook his head in amazement. "Do you know what would have happened if I'd called my mom stupid? She would have slapped me into the next county, that's what."

She crossed her arms. "Oh, so you're saying I should start slapping Jason around?"

"No, of course not."

"So what do you suggest I do?" Her tone was cool, but unmistakably angry.

"Demand that he show you respect. Stop mollycoddling him and start making him take some responsibility for himself."

"What makes you think I mollycoddle him?"

"An educated guess."

"Maybe I do, but he's my baby and he's only fifteen."

"Fifteen is no baby, Jinx. And he's certainly old enough to work." He sighed. "Look, you're not doing him any favors if you hand him everything. If he wants a motorcycle, let him earn it."

"You seem to be quite the authority on children. Strange, considering you have none of your own."

"No, I don't have any children; but I do have a master's degree in Adolescent Psychology."

"Oh." Suddenly Jenkins sagged.

"Jinx, you're tired, so I'm going to call a cab and get out of here." He pulled her into his embrace. "But I want to pick up where we left off this morning. As soon as possible."

"Ross, maybe we should just forget—" Her words were checked when he took her mouth in a wet, hungry kiss. And when his hand slid inside her robe to fondle her breast, she forgot what she was going to say anyway.

Finally he lifted his lips from hers and smiled. "I'll call you," he murmured. "Soon." And with a final light kiss on her cheek, he strode from the room.

* * *

It was after six when Jason finally returned home. He sauntered into the kitchen where Jenkins was stirring a pot of chili. "Hi, honey," she said.

Ignoring her greeting, he opened the refrigerator and peered inside.

"Jason, supper's almost ready. I've made your favorite, chili con carne." He still said nothing, and Jenkins sighed heavily. "Honey, please talk to me."

Wearing a sullen expression, Jason reached in the refrigerator and pulled out a half-gallon carton of milk, opened it, and turned it up to his mouth,

"Jason," Jenkins snapped. "How many times have I told you not to drink from the carton?"

Jason replaced the milk in the refrigerator, and wiped his mouth with the back of his hand. Then he looked at her and belched. "I dunno," he said. "Does five thousand times sound about right?"

"Oh, how nice. You've managed to go from being Mr. Silent Treatment to Mr. Smart-mouth in less than five minutes."

"Cut the crap, mom," Jason sneered.

Jenkins turned off the stove and walked over to the table. "Jason, I've had just about enough of your surly attitude. It's about time you remember that I am your mother and you owe me some respect."

Arms crossed, Jason slouched in his chair and stared sullenly at his shoes. Jenkins pulled out a chair and sat across from him.

"Jason, look at me." He raised his eyes and glowered at her. "Tell me what your father said."

"He didn't say anything because I didn't see him."

"You didn't?"

"No. He was in some kind of meeting," he snapped.

Jenkins bit her lip. Damn Jake, she thought, couldn't he have taken at least five minutes to see his only child? She'd seen the pain in Jason's eyes just now and was reminded how much the divorce had hurt her son.

Jason had changed enormously in the eighteen months since Jake walked out on them. At first, Jason had displayed his pain and confusion in the obvious ways. His grades dropped, he became surly and uncooperative, and had even been suspended from school for a week for fighting. That incident was the reason Jason was now attending a military school an hour from home. Jason needed discipline, Jake had insisted, and it would be better for everyone if he attended SMI for at least two years.

Jason, ready to do anything if it would gain his father's approval, agreed. Surprisingly, he was doing quite well at the institute and except for a few isolated incidents like today's, Jenkins was beginning to see traces of the old Jason.

"Look," Jenkins said quietly. "I'll make a deal with you about the motorcycle."

Jason looked at her, a glimmer of hope in his eyes. "What kind of deal?"

"I don't like the idea of your riding those things—"

"Mom, they aren't—" He stopped short when Jenkins held up her hand.

"I don't like the idea of your riding a motorcycle," she continued, "but I realize that you're practically a man now, and not a little boy." She bit her lip. "So here's the deal. I'll go with you to the bank for a loan—"

"Mom, that's super!"

"Wait a minute," she warned, "don't interrupt

until I'm finished. Your behavior this morning was unconscionable, and I don't want you to think for a minute that I will tolerate anything like that again. Nor do I want you to think that your tantrum had anything to do with my decision, because it didn't. Nevertheless, after you left, I began to rethink the situation and I realized that I might be wrong. And when I'm wrong, I admit it. However, before you get all excited, I want you to understand that there are some conditions to my allowing you to have a motorcycle."

"Anything, mom," Jason said, his voice harsh with controlled excitement. "I promise, I'll go along with whatever you say."

"We'll see. Here's the deal," Jenkins said, ticking each demand on her fingers. "First, you are going to start treating me with the respect I deserve. Second, you're going to pay for the motorcycle—which means you're going to have to get a job. I don't care what kind of job—mowing lawns, washing dishes, I don't care. But you are going to earn this motorcycle, Jason, do you understand?"

"Yes, ma'am."

"And there's one more thing. If you get a traffic ticket of any kind, the motorcycle will be parked for six full months and you'll have to get around on your bicycle. Understood?"

"Yes, ma'am."

"Good. Now go wash up while I put supper on the table."

Jason jumped up and started from the room. Then he turned around and walked to where Jenkins was ladling bowls of chili. He kissed her cheek. "Thanks, mom," he said.

"You're welcome, darling."

He shuffled his feet. "I'm really sorry I behaved like a jerk today. And I didn't mean it when I said you were stupid."

"You're forgiven. Now go wash up."

Later, as they sat down to supper, Jenkins decided to broach the subject of dating Ross to Jason. "Honey," she said, slowly stirring her chili. "You like Detective Tracy, don't you?"

"I guess so. It was real nice of him to drive us home from the police department the other night."

"Well, how would you feel—"

"Do you know what Kathy said, mom?" Jason interjected. He was laughing as he continued. "Kathy thinks you and the detective have something going between you."

"Oh?"

"Yeah, you know what I mean. She thinks you and Ross are having some kind of affair." Jason shoveled a spoonful of chili into his mouth and then took a long swallow of milk before continuing. "I told her that was crazy. Shoot, Detective Tracy could probably get a date with anyone he wanted to, so why would he be interested in you? Right, mom?"

Jenkins arched a brow at her son. "Gee, thanks."

He grinned sheepishly. "Aw, I didn't mean that like it sounded. What I meant was that Detective Tracy's way too young for you. Besides, you wouldn't be interested, would you, mom?"

Wondering how she should answer Jason's question, Jenkins picked up her empty bowl and put it in the sink. Now's the time to tell him, she thought. He's given me the perfect opening so all I have to do is tell him the truth.

"You wouldn't be interested, would you, mom?" he repeated.

Jenkins turned and saw the familiar haunted look in Jason's eyes, and she knew now wasn't the time for confessions. Instead, she made light of his question and answered him in the quavering voice of an octogenarian.

"Heavens to Betsy, sonny. Why if I tried to keep up with that young whippersnapper, I'd probably end up breaking my hip. You know how it is with us old folks—one false move and it's Wheelchair City."

Jason found her little act absolutely hysterical, and he laughed long and loud. Jenkins was glad he didn't notice the telltale disappointment in her eyes.

Eleven

Jenkins walked through the kitchen and her gaze fell on the leather bomber jacket hanging on the chair where Ross left it. He had to know the jacket was here, so why hadn't he returned for it?

Maybe he was staying away because he'd had second thoughts about last night—or, more specifically, this morning. God knew she'd had second, and even third, thoughts about it. She still had trouble believing what had happened between them. Or rather, she silently amended, what had almost happened. She must have been out of her mind to let things go so far.

In retrospect, she was immensely grateful for Jason's untimely arrival. Ross was too handsome and too charming by half, and she would have been worse than a fool to rush headlong into an intimate relationship with him. Intimacy was something Jenkins didn't take lightly and, as far as she was concerned, it was something that should be preceded by commitment—a word that she seriously doubted Detective Tracy liked.

She'd known from the first that Ross wasn't interested in long-term relationships. He'd told her as much the night they were strung up in the meat locker. Besides, she reminded herself, she didn't want a long-term relationship either. In fact, she didn't want a relationship at all. What was the saying, once burned, twice shy? She sighed. All this would be so much easier if she could just get the man out of her mind and heart.

The trill of the telephone interrupted her thoughts.

"Hello?"

"Hi, Jinx, it's Ross."

The mere sound of his voice made her heart skip. Unbidden, detailed images of this morning caused a telltale flush on her cheeks. Fighting to keep her jumbled emotions out of her voice, she cleared her throat. "Oh, hi, Ross, how are you?" she asked, hoping she sounded somewhat normal.

"Fine. Listen, you like Mel Gibson, don't you?"

"Um, yes, I like him. Why?"

"Because his new movie is playing at the Greensprings theater tonight. Want to go see it?"

Jenkins closed her eyes. Be strong, she silently lectured, you know it's for the best. "I can't, Ross, but thank you."

He was silent for a moment. "It's playing tomorrow night, too. We could go then."

"No, I don't think so. But thanks, anyway."

"What's wrong?"

Jenkins massaged her throbbing temples. "I don't think we should see each other again. You're a nice guy, but—"

"At least tell me why."

"You know why."

"Jason?"

"Yes."

There was a long pause, and then Ross asked, "Is Jason there? If he is, I'd like to speak with him."

Jenkins frowned. "You want to talk with Jason?"

"Yes, is it all right?"

"Why?"

Ross chuckled. "Do you always screen your son's calls?"

"No, of course not," she retorted. "Just a minute and I'll call him." She held the phone to her chest. "Jason! Telephone."

"I'll get it back here, mom," he called from his room. In a moment Jenkins heard his voice on the other line. "I've got it." There was a pause, and then, "Mom?"

"Yes?"

"You can hang up now."

"Oh, of course. Sorry." Jenkins fought the urge to listen to her son's conversation with Ross. What on earth could he be saying to Jason? She slowly hung up the phone.

Ten minutes later, Jason sauntered into the kitchen. "What did Detective Tracy want to talk to you about, honey?" Jenkins asked in a voice she hoped sounded nonchalant.

"He invited me over to his place," Jason said,

opening the refrigerator and taking out a carton of milk. Jenkins smiled when she saw him get a glass from the cabinet instead of drinking from the carton. She waited for him to say more, and when he didn't she asked, "Why did he ask you to his apartment?"

"He remembered that I was writing a paper for my criminal justice class and he offered to help me with it." Jason glanced up at her. "I can't believe he remembered. He seems like a really nice guy, mom."

Jenkins looked thoughtful. "Yes," she said, trying to keep suspicion out of her voice. "He certainly does."

"Oh, and he asked me to bring his jacket."

Jenkins slid her fingers over the smooth leather. "I'd wondered how I was going return it to him."

Jason popped a frozen waffle in the toaster. "Mom, do you ever think about you and dad getting back together?"

She snatched her fingers off the jacket. "Your father and I are divorced."

"I know that, but do you ever think about it? I mean, if dad wanted to come back to live with us, would you let him?"

Jenkins pulled out a chair and sat down. "Honey, Jake has made a new life with Carol. He won't be asking to come back."

Jason brought his plate of waffles and glass of milk to the table and sat down. "I'm just saying 'what if.' I mean, if things were different and dad wasn't with Carol. What if he realized he'd made a mistake and wanted to come back? Would you let him?"

"But he *is* with Carol, Jay."

Jason set down his glass so hard Jenkins was surprised it didn't shatter. "Mom!" His voice cracked with frustration. "You're not listening to me. I said, what if he *wasn't* living with her. What would you do?"

She frowned at her son. "Why? Has your father indicated—"

Jason clenched his hands into fists. "No, mom, dad hasn't said anything. I'm just asking, that's all."

Jenkins sighed. She was so very tired of playing this, or some variation of the "what if" game. She always tried to answer him as honestly as she could, but she was never sure if she were saying the right thing.

"Jason, I guess that if things were different, *if* your father could really change into a loving, faithful husband, and *if* he wanted to come back, I might consider giving our marriage another chance." She reached over and touched his fist. "But, honey, that's not going to happen."

"Yeah? Well, you never know."

The next day Jenkins, wearing Jason's old football jersey and a pair of faded jeans, was lying with her head and shoulders under the kitchen sink. As she tried to loosen the grease trap she heard Jason enter the house. "Mom? Where are you?" he called.

"I'm in the kitchen, Jason, would you come give me a hand?" She heard the squeak of his sneakers on the kitchen floor. "I can't reach the wrench, honey, would you hand it to me, please?" She blindly waved her hand and in a moment she felt the weight of the heavy tool in her open palm. "Thanks, darling," she said.

"Anytime, sweetheart," replied a deep voice.

Startled, Jenkins sat up, banging her head on a pipe in the process. "Ow!" she grumbled as she slid out from under the sink and, rubbing the top of her head, looked up. "Ross, what are you doing here? I thought we agreed not to see each other anymore."

"I don't remember agreeing to anything. Besides Jason invited me, so what was I to do?"

She sighed. "You could have told him no."

"And hurt the kid's feelings?"

"You could have said you had other plans," she argued.

"You wanted me to lie to your own flesh and blood?" His expression of horror was a bit melodramatic and Jenkins had to force herself not to smile.

He sat on the floor beside her. "Can I help with that?" he asked before she could think of a response.

If only he didn't look so incredibly . . . incredible Jenkins thought. It was hard to even think with him sitting beside her. She shook her head and tried to ignore her growing attraction for the charming detective.

"I dropped my ring down the drain and I was trying to retrieve it from the grease trap."

Ross glanced at the floor and then chuckled softly as he picked something up. He held up the object. "Could this be the ring you were looking for?"

Jenkins's mouth dropped open. "Do you mean it was on the floor all the time?"

"Apparently so.

Jenkins blew an errant curl from her eyes. "I'm glad you found it instead of Jason. He'd never let me live this down." She frowned and looked around. "Speaking of Jason, where is he?"

"He's test-driving my motorcycle."

"What?" She rose on her knees to try to look out the window.

"He told me about the deal you two made. I figured that if he's going to buy a motorcycle, he should get a good one. My bike is over twenty years old, but it's in excellent condition and I quoted him a fair price."

"B-but. . . ." She started to stand.

Ross grabbed her wrist. "He's all right, Jinx. He's wearing a helmet and he's only going to ride it around the neighborhood." He fell back on the floor and drew her down with him. "Now come here and kiss me before Jason gets back and I have to start behaving like Detective Tracy again."

Lying atop him, her body perfectly aligned with his and knowing she was probably going to regret it, Jenkins allowed him to kiss her—and she kissed him back.

"Jinx," Ross said when finally he broke the long and satisfying kiss. "When can I see you again?"

"I told you, I don't think it's a good idea." Jenkins didn't sound convincing even to herself. She started to rise, but Ross held her firmly against his chest.

"Stay where you are for a minute and listen to me. I like you, Jinx, and I think you like me. Or am I mistaken about that?"

She frowned at him. "You know I like you, but I explained—"

"I know, you're afraid of hurting Jason. But what's wrong with our spending time together when he's away at school?"

Jenkins rolled off Ross's chest and lay with her head resting on his muscled arm. "Because I think your idea of spending time together and my idea of it are very different."

He raised up so he could see her face. "Why, because I want to make love with you?"

She shook her head. "Yes, because you want to have sex with me."

"I said want to make love with you, not have sex with you. There is a difference."

She sighed and closed her eyes. "Oh, Ross, there's no sense in arguing semantics."

Ross seemed to study her. "Jinx, there *is* a difference."

Jenkins shrugged. "Okay, whatever you say."

Seeming to realize that she did not believe him, he changed the subject. "Okay, how about this: will you let me stay for supper?"

"Don't you work anymore?" she said petulantly.

"Yeah, but I work nights, remember? I don't go on until ten o'clock."

"Oh."

He ran his finger over the bridge of her nose. "I just want to talk, Jinx."

"I don't see that there's anything left to talk about."

"I think there is."

Jenkins looked at him. "Jason will be here."

"I know that, and I certainly don't mind. I like Jason."

"Really? I seem to remember your calling him a brat."

Ross grimaced. "Well, sometimes he is. But under all that anger and frustration is a pretty great kid."

Jenkins studied him a moment. "I almost believe you mean that."

"I do mean it." Ross shook his head. "Jinx, to your knowledge have I ever lied to you about anything?"

"No, as far as I know, you've been quite open with me."

"Exactly. So, what'll it be? May I stay for supper?"

Part of her wanted to say yes and the other part of her knew she was entering dangerous ground. After what had almost happened the other morning, Jenkins knew she couldn't trust herself to remain in control where Ross Tracy was concerned.

Filled with uncertainty, she chewed her lip as she considered the situation. One thing was certain. With Jason in the same room, Ross could hardly set about seducing her.

"All right, you can stay for supper, but it'll be just friends having a nice evening together."

"Hey, I like being your friend. S'okay with me."

The sound of a motorcycle broke the stillness and Ross smiled wryly. "Better get up, Mrs. McGraw, unless you want to explain to your son why we're sprawled on the kitchen floor."

Twelve

All during supper Jenkins listened while Ross and Jason talked about everything from sports to the weather—and, of course, motorcycles. She hadn't realized how much she'd missed having a meal at the table instead of in front of the television, as she and Jason were wont to do since the divorce.

She'd insisted that this supper be simply a friendly get-together, and Ross was cooperating. He was the perfect guest: considerate, interesting, soft-spoken. In fact, tonight Ross was behaving as the perfect role model for Jason.

Jenkins sighed inwardly. Every time she looked at him her insides seemed to melt. How was it that he could do that to her with one smile, one wink? Though it was true that he was incredibly handsome, it wasn't his appearance that made her go all mushy. It was that he was a genuinely nice man and, more importantly, he treated Jason like someone who mattered. When Ross asked Jason's opinion, he really listened to the boy's responses. And Jason relished the attention.

This isn't good, Jenkins thought grimly. It would be so easy to fall in love with Ross—and she wasn't absolutely sure she wasn't past that point already.

"Where are you, Jinx?"

Jenkins blinked. "I'm sorry, what did you say?"

Ross took her hand. "You seemed a million miles away."

She shrugged and laughed self-consciously. "I'm afraid I was woolgathering."

Ross winked. "We've bored your mother. Too much guy talk."

"Yeah, I guess so," Jason replied. "Sorry, mom."

"That's all right." She eased her fingers from Ross's grasp. "Would anyone care for dessert?"

"Not me, thanks," Ross said.

"None for me, either. I've gotta go, mom, I prom- ised Kathy I'd take her to a hay ride the Caldwells are having. We're going to ride out there with Sean Reilly and his girlfriend." He wiped his mouth and threw his napkin on the table. Then he pushed back his chair and stood, "Is it okay if I spend the night at Sean's? Dad's taking me back to school in the morning."

"Did Sean's mom say it was okay?"

"Yes, ma'am."

"All right, but you must first call your father and make arrangements for him to pick you up at Sean's. Your clothes are already packed, so don't forget to take them with you when you leave."

"Thanks, mom. I'll go call dad now." He looked at his watch. "Yikes, Sean's supposed to pick me up in about ten minutes." He started to leave the room and stopped, turning back toward Ross. "Thanks for helping me with my paper. I'll let you know what kind of grade I make on it."

"You do that."

"And as soon as mom and I work things out, I'd like to discuss buying your Harley."

"It'll be there when you're ready for it. I'm sort of attached to that old hog. I prefer that she go to a good home."

Jason grinned. "Don't worry, I'll take good care of her."

A few minutes later Jason was heading out the door. "Sean's here," he called. "See ya next weekend, Mom."

"Bye, darling. See you next weekend." The front door slammed and Jenkins shook her head. Then, she looked at Ross. "Thank you for being so nice to Jason today."

"I enjoyed the time with him. He's really bright, you know?"

Jenkins smiled. "I know, but I appreciate your saying it."

Ross slid his chair back from the table. "That was a great supper, Jinx," he said, pushing up his sleeves. "And since you cooked, I'll do the dishes."

"All right."

He glanced at her, a look of mild surprise on his face. "That's okay with you?"

Jenkins arched a brow. "If you're hoping I'll say no, you're going to be disappointed." She waved her hand toward the table. "Go ahead, have at it."

"You mean you aren't going to insist on doing the dishes yourself?"

She chuckled. "Do I seem stupid to you? Not on your life, big guy. And since you were kind enough to offer to do the dishes, I think I'll sit down, prop my feet up, and have a cup of coffee. It's been a long day and I'm suddenly very tired."

Ross rinsed the last of the dishes and put them in the dishwasher, wiped off the countertops, the stove, and the table, and swept the kitchen floor. Finished, he rolled down his shirtsleeves and went in search of Jinx. The large family room adjoined the kitchen and he found her lying on the sofa.

"The kitchen's done," he said, walking up beside her. "Jinx?" She was asleep. He watched her for a moment and noted the slight rise and fall of the empty coffee cup balanced on her chest.

Smiling, Ross reached down and fingered a silken, copper-colored curl that fell across her cheek. God, he thought. He'd like to pick her up in his arms and carry her straight back to the bedroom. He wondered if he dared. Then, glancing at his watch, Ross sighed. It was nearly nine o'clock. If he expected to get to work on time, he'd better leave, pronto.

Taking care not to wake her, Ross removed the coffee cup from Jenkins's chest and took it to the sink. Then, he picked up an afghan that lay folded across the back of the sofa and spread it over Jenkins's sleeping form. That done, he pulled on his jacket, turned off all the lights save a small lamp in the family room, and let himself out the garage door.

The grandfather clock in the foyer chimed and Jenkins groaned, rolled over, and promptly fell off the sofa. She sat up immediately and looked around. Disoriented, it took her a full minute to realize where she was and to get untangled from the afghan twisted around her legs. She remembered lying down on the sofa—she had intended to rest only a moment and then help Ross with the kitchen. She hadn't really meant to make him do it all, but she must have fallen asleep.

Jenkins sighed. Poor Ross, he'd not only been left to clean the kitchen, but he'd even had to see himself out. Some hostess she was, she thought wryly as she got to her feet. She would have to apologize the next time she saw him. If there was a next time.

Jenkins yawned and stretched, then looked at her watch and saw that it was almost seven-thirty. It was Tish's turn to prepare Sunday breakfast and if Jenkins expected to eat at eight then she'd better head to the shower now. She folded the afghan and replaced it on the back of the sofa, then headed for the laundry room to get a stack of towels.

She was humming when she opened the door, but the tune ended abruptly when a tattooed hand closed over her wrist and jerked her further inside.

"Surprise."

Terrified, Jenkins stared at the armed intruder as she backed against the washing machine. "H-how did you get in my house?" she whispered.

Ray Price grinned. "It was easy." He pointed the pistol over her shoulder. "I just climbed in through that little ol' window right there behind you." He snickered. "Don't you know it's dangerous not to lock your windows, Miz McGraw?" His face turned hard. "I just been waitin' for the right time to break in. I been watchin' your house for a long, long time."

"Why?"

" 'Cause you're the reason I got to hide from the law. If you'da kept your mouth shut, nobody woulda knowed I was the one that robbed that store. I shoulda killed you when I had the chance."

Jenkins swallowed and licked her suddenly dry lips. "Are you going to kill me now?"

"Naw, leastwise not yet. I got other plans for you."

"What do you want? Money? I don't have much cash, but you can have whatever I've got."

"Oh, I'll git your money, Miz McGraw. And I'll git your car, too, 'cause me and you is gonna take a little trip. But right now, I'm hungry and you're gonna fix me something to eat."

Jenkins swallowed nervously. A trip? To where? "All right." Stall, she thought. Do whatever it takes to stall him. "What would you like? Breakfast?"

He grinned, showing, surprisingly strong, perfect teeth. "Yeah. Make me a breakfast with all the trimmin's."

Jenkins nodded. "Okay. Then let's go to the kitchen."

Price opened the door and motioned for her to precede him. Heart in her throat, Jenkins walked through the door and into the kitchen. She moved slowly and deliberately, afraid that any sudden movement would startle the man into firing the gun pointed at her.

Ray Price settled on one of the high stools at the counter and watched Jenkins move about the kitchen. "I like my eggs over easy," he said when she took the carton from the refrigerator. "And the bacon better be crisp."

"All right." Jenkins opened a drawer to remove a spatula and a pill bottle rolled into view. Jenkins stared at it. Shortly after Jake had walked out on her, Jenkins had suffered with insomnia. The bottle contained medicine that her doctor had prescribed to help her sleep.

Dare she try to slip some of it in Ray Price's food?

"I want biscuits, too."

His voice startled her out of her reverie. "I-I can't make biscuits, I'm out of flour. How about toast, or English muffins?"

As she spoke, she stealthily opened the bottle of pills and quietly spilled its contents in the bottom of the drawer. Ray was looking elsewhere when she looked up and she managed to pocket several capsules.

"Toast. You got grits?"

"I think so—" Jenkins froze as the telephone be-

gan to ring. It had to be Tish calling about breakfast.
If she didn't answer the phone, Tish was bound to
come and investigate, and she certainly didn't want
her best friend walking into this dangerous situation.

She looked anxiously at Ray Price. "That's probably my neighbor calling. We always eat breakfast
together on Sunday. If I don't answer it she'll know
something's wrong."

He motioned toward the phone. "Answer it, but
don't try anything stupid."

Jenkins nodded and picked up the receiver. Then,
taking a deep, calming breath, she said, "Hello?"

"Your breakfast is getting cold, Jenkins," Tish
said. "You'd better hurry up."

"Oh. Well, I'm not feeling well this morning, Tish.
I'm going to have to bow out this time."

"What's the matter?"

Jenkins licked her lips nervously. "I-I think I'm
coming down with a cold."

"Oh, I'm sorry. Anything I can do?"

Suddenly she had an idea. "Yes." Jenkins took a
deep breath. Please, she thought, let Tish understand what I'm about to say. "If you happen to talk
to Ross Dylan, tell him I finally found those Wayfarers he was looking for. They were right here under
my nose."

"What? Who's Ross Dylan?" Tish asked, obviously
confused.

"You know how he loves those high-priced sunglasses. He's been looking for them for weeks."

"Jenkins, what are you talking about?"

Ray Price narrowed his eyes suspiciously and motioned for her to get off the phone. "Um, I've gotta

go, Tish. I'll talk to you later." Jenkins quickly disconnected the call and looked nervously at Price.

"You did real good," he said. "Now hurry up with my breakfast. We've got a long day ahead of us."

Tish slowly replaced the receiver in its cradle and looked at her husband. "That was the strangest telephone conversation I've ever had."

"Oh?"

"Buzzy, do you know anybody named Ross Dylan?"

"No. Can't say that I do."

"Neither do I, but Jenkins asked me to give him a message." She sat down at the breakfast table. "Buzzy, something's just not right. It was almost as if Jenkins were talking to me in some kind of code." She chewed her lip. "Ross Dylan, Ross Dylan. I've heard that name somewhere, but I can't remember— Wait a minute! R.D. Tracy! Ross Dylan Tracy! Buzzy, I think Jenkins was giving me a message for Detective Tracy!"

Thirteen

Ross and Kelly were at the station finishing some paperwork when the call came in. Kelly answered it, then looked at his partner.

"Ross, this is for you. Somebody named Tish Armstrong?"

Ross, his eyes feeling gritty from lack of sleep, nodded tiredly and picked up the extension at his desk. He wondered why Jinx's friend was calling him. "Tracy here."

"Ross, I think Jenkins may be in some kind of trouble."

Immediately alert, his exhaustion forgotten, Ross pressed the phone more tightly against his ear. "What kind of trouble?"

"I'm not sure. All I know is that I just had a strange telephone conversation with her and she asked me to give a message to Ross Dylan. Isn't that your name?"

"Yeah, it is. But why . . . never mind. What's the message?"

"That's the strange part. She said if I saw you I was to tell you that she found the sunglasses you were looking for."

"What? I haven't been looking for any sunglasses."

Tish sighed. "I was afraid you'd say that."

"What else did she say, Tish?"

"That's it, that's all she said. I told you it was strange."

Ross leaned back in his chair and rubbed his forehead. "This doesn't make any sense. Are you sure that's all she said?"

"I'm positive. Ross, something's wrong, I just know it. I think she was trying to tell me something and couldn't. I got the feeling she wasn't alone. Do you think I should send Buzzy over there to check on her?"

Ross felt his gut tighten. "No, don't do that. Let's go over this message again. Tell me exactly what she said, word for word, and don't leave anything out."

Tish explained how she and Jenkins routinely took turns making Sunday breakfast. "Today was my turn. Jenkins was late, so I phoned to tell her breakfast was getting cold. She said she thought she was coming down with a cold. I asked her if there was anything I could do, and she said, 'Yes, if you see Ross Dylan, tell him I finally found those Wayfarers he's been looking for. They were right under my nose.' And then she said, 'You know how he loves those high-priced sunglasses, he's been looking for them for weeks.' After that, she said she had to go and hung up."

Ross frowned. The whole thing sounded crazy. "Hold on a minute, Tish." He looked over at his partner. "Kelly, do you know anything about Wayfarer sunglasses?"

Kelly shrugged. "I know they're made by Ray-Ban and are pretty expensive, why?"

"Ray-Ban," Ross murmured, "Ray-Ban, high-priced sunglasses. What could she have meant by—" He sat up abruptly. "Holy Christ! Tish, I know what Jinx was trying to tell me."

Ray Price took the last bite of his breakfast and pushed back the plate. "Pretty good breakfast." He grunted appreciatively, and picked his teeth with the edge of a matchbook.

"W-would you like some more coffee?"

He grinned. "I believe I would." He glanced out the window of the back door and frowned. "What's going on at your neighbors? Sure are a lot of cars over there."

Jenkins looked out and saw the driveway at Tish's

house was congested with cars and, unless she was mistaken, one of them was Ross's red sports car. For the first time since Ray Price had appeared, she felt a glimmer of hope. Tish had understood.

"Oh, they have a new baby," she lied. "Must be people dropping by to welcome the little fellow."

Price walked to the door and peered out. While his attention was diverted, Jenkins quickly poured the contents of five of the sleeping capsules in the bottom of his cup and then filled it with the dark brew. Price walked back to the counter.

"Where's my coffee?" he snapped.

"Coming right up," she said. "You said you like cream and lots of sugar, right?"

"Right."

Jenkins stirred in a non-dairy creamer along with three heaping spoons of sugar, silently praying that the sugar would mask the taste of the medicine.

"Here you go," she said, setting the cup of coffee on the counter in front of Price.

Jenkins nervously watched him sip the coffee. Would he notice the medicine this time? She'd doctored his first cup and he hadn't noticed, but she hadn't put in as much and he'd been eating, too.

He slurped the coffee. "What time is it?" he asked.

Jenkins looked at her watch, "Almost nine."

He turned up the cup and swallowed down the last of the drugged coffee. "We gotta get movin'," he said, "we got a long ways to go."

"Now? Wouldn't it be better to leave after dark?" Jenkins stalled. How long would it take for the medicine to kick in? She'd given him enough to fell a horse, or so she thought.

"Naw. We're gonna leave now. Get your car keys."

"It's cold outside. I'll need my coat," she said.

"Then git it, and let's git moving."

Jenkins got her coat and took her car keys off the hook by the door. She held the keys out to him.

"You drive," Price said, shaking his head as if to clear it. "I ain't feelin' so good." He motioned toward the door leading to the garage. "Let's go."

Jenkins walked out to the garage and got inside the car. Price kept the gun trained on her as he walked around the car and entered it on the passenger-side. "Mind if I turn on the heater?" Jenkins asked.

"Turn it on," he growled. "And let's get outta here." He narrowed his eyes at her. "I'm warnin' you, lady, don't do anything that would draw no cops' attention, you hear? You do and I'll make you wish you was dead."

Jenkins nodded. She carefully backed the car out of the garage and drove slowly down the quiet street. At the stop sign she looked at Price. "Which way?" she asked.

"Whichever's the quickest way to I-59," he said.

Jenkins turned to the right and then right again at the next street. By leaving the subdivision this route she would pass Tish's house and maybe someone would see her. There were cars everywhere, but Jenkins didn't see a single person as she drove past.

"Can't you go any faster?"

"I'm going the speed limit. You said not to—"

"Yeah, yeah, okay." Price rested his head on the

back of the seat. "Damn, I feel bad. I'm gettin' all woozy."

"You're probably just tired," Jenkins murmured. "How long has it been since you slept?"

"Been a while," he replied, rubbing his eyes with the back of his hand. "Sleepin' and runnin' from the law don't mix." He chuckled at his little joke.

"I see what you mean," she said, smiling weakly. Jenkins glanced in the rearview mirror and saw the familiar red sports car following about two car lengths behind. Ross. Thank God.

"Where are we going?" she asked.

"That's something you'll know when I'm ready to tell you. Right now you just drive to the interstate."

Jenkins noticed that Price's speech was beginning to slur. The medicine was apparently doing its work. Out of the corner of her eye, Jenkins cast furtive glances at Price. He yawned twice and smacked his lips. Then, his eyelids began to droop and he didn't seem to notice when the gun slipped from his fingers with a muffled thump. In a moment Ray Price was snoring.

"Finally," Jenkins muttered under her breath. She looked over at him. "Ray?" she said hesitantly. "Ray, you awake?" He didn't respond, he didn't even move. Good, he's dead to the world, she thought grimly as she turned the car toward town. She hoped she hadn't killed him.

Twenty minutes later she parked in front of the police station and eased out of the car. At the same time the red sports car skidded to a stop behind her. Ross jumped from it and ran toward her.

"Jinx," he said, pulling her against him. "Christ, are you all right? Where's Price?"

"In the car, sleeping like a baby."

"He's what?" Ross bent to peer through the car's window. "I don't believe this. He really is asleep." He motioned to several policemen, and he and Jenkins watched as the officers quickly took a dazed and befuddled Price into custody.

When they had half-dragged, half-carried Price inside, Ross looked at Jenkins, amazement on his face. "What happened to him?"

Jenkins grinned wickedly. "I gave him coffee laced with sleeping pills."

"You drugged him?"

Jenkins nodded. "Guilty as charged, Your Honor. As a matter of fact, you máy want to have a doctor look at him. I'm not exactly sure how much of the sleeping powder he might have ingested. I think I must have emptied at least seven or eight of the capsules into his coffee."

Ross bracketed her face with his hands and kissed her soundly. "Jenkins McGraw," he said, "You are a remarkable woman."

Once again, Jenkins found herself in Lieutenant Chuck Llewellyn's office answering questions about Ray Price.

The lieutenant read Ross's preliminary report and, smiling, he shook his head. "Mrs. McGraw, this is unbelievable. While Price was holding a pistol on you, you actually managed to get your friend to call Detective Tracy and tell him Ray Price was in your house?"

"Yes, sir. I wasn't sure Tish would understand what

I was saying, I could only pray that she, or Ross . . . er . . . Detective Tracy, would figure it out."

"What exactly did you say to Mrs. Armstrong?"

"I told her to tell Ross Dylan that I'd found his Wayfarer sunglasses in my house."

The lieutenant looked up at Ross. "And from *that* you figured out that Ray Price was holding Mrs. McGraw hostage?"

Ross grinned. "Yes, sir."

"How?"

"Well, you see—"

"Never mind," Lieutenant Llewellyn said, holding up his hand. "You can put it all in your final report. Right now I think you should take Mrs. McGraw home. I expect she's tired."

"Show me how Price got inside your house, Jinx," Ross said the moment they entered through the garage.

"Through the laundry room," she replied, leading the way. "The window wasn't locked and all he had to do was cut the screen. He got in because of my stupidity. I always open the window when I do laundry." She slammed the window shut and locked it. "I won't make that mistake again." She shook her head.

Ross put his arm around her shoulders. "You're exhausted. I'll leave so you can get some sleep."

Jenkins hugged herself. "Would you mind staying long enough for me to take a quick shower? I mean, I know Ray Price is behind bars and all, but I'm feeling a little unnerved right now." She gave him a weak smile. "Post-traumatic shock, I suppose."

"Sure," Ross said, giving her arm a squeeze. "I won't go anywhere until you feel safe enough to be left alone."

"Thanks." She reached to the stack of folded towels atop the dryer. "I'll try to make it quick."

"Take as long as you need," he said. "I'm in no hurry."

Jenkins reached into the shower and turned on the water. While steam filled the small bathroom, she peeled off her jeans and sweatshirt and stepped under the torrent of water. Turning her face up to the hot, steaming spray, she finally let go of the emotions she'd held back since finding Ray Price in her laundry room. She'd been so terrified he was going to kill her. Now that she was safe, she could allow herself the luxury of tears. As the hot water poured over her, Jenkins began to sob.

The door to the bathroom eased open. "Jinx? You all right."

She heard the worry in Ross's voice and she tried to answer him, but she couldn't talk for crying. A few moments later the shower door opened and Ross, gloriously naked, stepped inside. Jenkins moved into his arms and Ross held her tenderly while she wept. Beneath the stinging spray, Ross whispered soft assurances that she was safe, that he wouldn't leave her.

Her tears spent, Jenkins stepped back and looked up at Ross. Seeing the genuine concern etched on his handsome face, all her defenses crumbled. There was no point in denying the truth any longer. She was in love with Ross Tracy. She touched his lips.

"Make love to me, Ross," she murmured.

Fourteen

At her soft request, Ross blinked away the water that clung to his lashes and swallowed thickly. God knew there was nothing he wanted more than to make love to this woman. His whole body ached with the desire to bury himself inside her, to feel her moving beneath him, to hear her tiny sighs of pleasure. But did she feel real desire for him, or did she simply need to be held?

"Ross?"

Ross stared down at the woman in his arms, searching her face for some sign that her request wasn't simply a reaction to the trauma of the past several hours. Jenkins had never looked more vulnerable as she did this moment—nor more appealing. Her copper hair was slicked back from her face; her skin, sprinkled with freckles and free of cosmetics, looked as youthful as a girl's. But her body, lithe and silky-sleek, was no girl's. The body in his arms was undeniably a woman's.

"Jinx, I don't . . . are you sure?"

She slid her hands up his chest and over his shoulders and leaned into him so that her breasts rubbed against his stomach.

"I've never been more sure of anything in my life," she murmured, flicking her tongue over his small male nipples to catch droplets of water on them.

Ross's breath caught. "Oh, Jinx." His hands were shaking as he slid them over her soft bottom. Heart pounding, he grasped the backs of her thighs and lifted her to straddle his hips.

She wrapped her legs around him, chuckling softly. "I've been here before," she said, huskily.

He grinned down at her as he recalled the night that seemed a lifetime ago. "I know. I've dreamed about it often enough."

"So have I. I've wanted this for so long, Ross, don't make me wait any longer."

With a groan of a man whose control was rapidly slipping, Ross took her mouth hungrily. She wriggled her body against his. "Make love to me, now, please," she panted, and he turned and held Jenkins against the slick tile wall. Splaying his large hands over her buttocks to hold her steady, Ross drove himself into her.

Jenkins quickly adjusted to the sensual rhythm of his hips, meeting each hard thrust with one of her own. There was no gentleness in their mating, no murmurs of love. There would be time for those things later. For now they were ruled by mutual need. Their joining was frenzied, fiery, their breathing coming in great gasps as together they appeased the desire that had consumed them almost from the moment they met.

When their passion was spent, Ross slowly eased Jenkins to her feet. Her legs, weak from the wild ride, trembled and she gripped the mounted hand rail for support. She watched through half-closed eyes as Ross picked up the oval bar of soap and

rubbed it between his large hands until thick, white
lather oozed between his fingers.

Without speaking he began to soap her body, beginning at her neck and shoulders, and then moving
down to circle over her breasts, her belly, her legs.
He knelt and lifted her foot, gently bathed it and
moved to the other. As he gently massaged her body,
her muscles seemed to turn to mush and if she
hadn't been gripping the handrail, she would have
melted at his feet.

When Ross finished washing every inch of her
with the sweet-smelling lather, he rinsed her, then
lifted her in his arms and stepped out of the shower.
He sat her on the toilet seat and then carefully and
lovingly wrapped her in a towel.

Jenkins was so relaxed that she was nearly asleep
when he led her into the bedroom. He threw back
the bed covers, helped her to lie down and then
tucked the sheets and blankets around her. She was
barely aware when he crawled in the bed beside her
and pulled her into the cradle of his hard body.

"Go to sleep, Jinx," he murmured. "I'll be right
here to watch over you."

Jenkins smiled sleepily. Since the day her ex-
husband Jake had walked out on her, she had been
forced to be the strong one, to be the protector,
the caretaker. This was the first time in a long,
long while that anyone had taken the time to pamper and protect her.

She yawned and snuggled deeper into her pillow.
I could get used to this, she thought. I could so
easily get used to this.

* * *

Jenkins had been sleeping soundly for nearly two hours when Ross eased out of bed and pulled the blankets more securely around her. Moving quietly so as not to awaken her, he pulled on his jeans and padded from the room and down the hall to the kitchen.

Ross put on a pot of coffee and then reached for the phone. He punched in the familiar number and listened for the distant ring. It only rang twice.

"Hello?"

"Kell, it's me."

"Ross, where in the hell are you? I've been calling your place for hours."

"I'm at Jinx's. She was still pretty shaken up when I brought her home, so I stayed with her."

There was a pause on the other end, and then, "I see."

Though Kelly only spoke two words, Ross heard the condemnation in his voice. "Just what, exactly, do you see?" he asked, gripping the receiver so hard it was a wonder it didn't crack.

Kelly sighed. "Nothing. Where's Mrs. McGraw now?"

"She's sleeping." Ross pushed his hand through his hair. "Kell, I know something's on your mind, so just say what's bugging you."

There was another long pause. "Look," his partner finally said. "It's none of my business, but . . ."

Ross felt his jaw tighten. "Go on."

"From the little I've seen of Mrs. McGraw, she seems like a really nice lady."

"Yes, she's a very nice lady. So?"

"But she's not exactly your usual type, Ross. She doesn't seem to be quite as, ah, worldly as the women who normally strike your fancy."

Ross leaned against the wall. "Where is this going, Kelly? Come on, spit it out."

Kelly sighed again. "I just don't think it's right to take advantage of someone like her, Ross."

"What's that supposed to mean?"

"Ross, you rarely stay in a relationship more than a month at most. But it never mattered because the women you picked weren't interested in more than a good time, either. But this lady doesn't strike me as the kind who changes bed partners as often as she changes sheets."

"Meaning I do?" Ross snapped.

Kelly chuckled. "In a word? Yes."

"Thanks, pal," Ross growled. "It's reassuring to know that you think so highly of me."

"Ross, you're my best friend, my partner. Dammit, I think the world of you and you know it. But I think you're letting your little head rule your big one, if you know what I mean. And I don't want to see that nice lady get hurt."

"I'm sure she'll be touched by your concern." Ross's voice dripped with sarcasm.

"Aw, hell," Kelly said, clearly exasperated. "Now you're mad. Look, just forget I said anything. It's none of my business. Where do you want me to pick you up tonight? Your place or Mrs. McGraw's?"

Ross rubbed his temples. "I'm not sure yet. I'll call you." He hung up the phone and stared at it for a long time.

Kelly was right about his past relationships; he hadn't found a woman who could hold his interest for more than a month. Ross looked toward the hall that led to the bedroom and Jinx. Would the same thing happen with Jinx a few weeks down the road?

He didn't know the answer to that one. If that happened, he could end up hurting her even more than her ex-husband had. Maybe Kelly was right about everything. Maybe the kindest thing he could do would be to bow out now before it was too late.

Then Ross remembered the scene in the shower and he closed his eyes. He hadn't intended for that to happen. He'd heard Jinx crying and without a second's hesitation he'd stripped off his clothes and gone to her. All he'd wanted to do, all he'd intended, was to give her comfort.

He rubbed his face. Oh, he'd given her comfort, all right. He'd taken her with no more thought or preparation than an animal. He'd known even then that he was only giving in to his physical needs. He was angry about the way he took her, too. He hadn't made love to her. In fact, there was no way he could call what he'd done making love. He'd screwed her, pure and simple. Jinx had been at her most vulnerable and he'd taken advantage of the fact. And, to make matters worse, he'd been irresponsible as hell. He hadn't even used a condom!

He felt lower than pond scum.

Jenkins woke slowly. She blinked at the clock on her bedside table. Good heavens, it was after five o'clock. She'd slept the entire day away. She threw back the covers and sat up, wincing when the sore muscles on the inside of her thighs complained. The phrase *saddle sore* came to mind as she slowly pulled herself to her feet, and she grinned wryly. It pretty much described how she felt. It had, after all, been a wild ride.

She was wondering where Ross was when she heard the faint rattle of dishes. She smiled to herself as she pulled on her robe. In the kitchen, of course. It was late and he was probably hungry by now. She belted her thick terrycloth robe and padded down the hall.

"I hope you've made coffee," she called as she walked through the den toward the kitchen.

"Got a fresh pot brewin' as we speak," said a feminine voice.

Jenkins paused. "Tish?"

Tish's pert blond head peeked around the door. "Yeah?"

"Are you the only one here?"

Tish nodded. "Ross called me a couple of hours ago and asked me to come over. He didn't want you to wake up and find yourself all alone."

Jenkins walked into the kitchen and sat down at the table. "That was nice of him," she murmured. Couldn't he at least have said, good-bye?

Tish seemed to sense what her friend was thinking. She poured a mug of coffee and placed it in Jenkins's hands. "He had to go to work, sweetie," she said, sitting across from her. "He didn't want to disturb your rest. You had a pretty harrowing morning."

Jenkins sipped her coffee and then carefully set the cup on the table. "Did he say anything?"

Tish cocked her head. "About what?"

Jenkins shook her head and stared down at her coffee. I'm so stupid, she thought with disgust. Did she really think that Ross would have discussed what had happened between them with Tish?

"I figured you'd be hungry when you woke, so I made some spaghetti. Shall I fix your plate?"

Jenkins looked at her friend's concerned face. She wasn't the least bit hungry, but she didn't have the heart to say so.

"That sounds great. I'd love some."

"Coming right up." Tish jumped up from the table. "I've got some garlic bread ready for the oven. As soon as it's toasted, you can eat."

Jenkins watched Tish flutter about the kitchen. "I haven't thanked you for calling the police for me. I know you must have thought I was crazy when we spoke this morning."

Tish laughed. "I'll admit I was thrown for a couple of seconds. Nothing you said made any sense and that's how I knew something was wrong. I talk non-sense all the time, but you don't. I'll admit, though, it took me a minute to realize that Ross Dylan was Ross Tracy."

She shoved the pan of bread in the oven and then sat back down at the table. "That thing about the sunglasses was brilliant. Whatever made you think of it?"

Jenkins shrugged. "I remembered Jason's begging me for a pair of Wayfarers last summer and the idea just popped in my head. I wasn't sure you'd under-stand what I was trying to tell you, though, or Ross, either, for that matter."

"Well, he did. He's a good cop."

Jenkins looked at her hands. "Yeah," she said, softly. "He's a good cop."

Tish reached across the table and touched her hand. "Jenkins? Is there something you need to talk about? Did Ray Price . . . did he hurt you?"

Jenkins squeezed Tish's hand. "No, other than scaring me out of my wits, he didn't hurt me. He's not very bright, thank goodness. He blamed me for his being in trouble with the law, and as punishment he was going to make me drive him somewhere." She shook her head. "He never said where we were going. Or what he was going to do with me when we got there."

She shuddered, and picked up her mug of coffee. "I'm glad I didn't have to find out."

"So am I." Tish looked toward the oven. "I think the bread's ready."

"Did Ross say whether or not he'd need me anymore . . . in regard to the case, I mean?" Jenkins asked as Tish filled a plate with noodles and sauce.

Tish didn't reply until she set the steaming plate of spaghetti on the table. "No, he didn't say. But if he needs you again, I'm sure he'll call and let you know."

If. Funny how such a tiny word could sound so significant, Jenkins mused as she sipped her coffee.

Fifteen

He didn't call. Not the next day, nor the day after, nor the day after that. And when she didn't hear from him on the fifth day, Jenkins knew Ross wasn't going to call. And worse, she was pretty sure she knew the reason.

Who could blame him? She'd been the one who'd insisted they could be no more than friends. And he'd agreed, albeit reluctantly at first. And look what happened. At the first opportunity she'd thrown herself at him; she'd all but demanded that he make love to her.

And what had he done? He'd hesitated. That moment's hesitation should have told her that his feelings had changed. But she'd insisted. What had she been thinking? She'd never been wishy-washy before, why now? What must Ross think of a women who was cold one minute and hot the next; a woman who said she wanted only friendship, and in less than twenty-four hours was begging him to make love to her. And she'd had to beg. She flushed at the memory.

So he'd taken her in the shower without preamble, almost as if he were angry. And, she thought remorsefully, when all was said and done, he'd had every right to be angry.

Jason came home that Saturday full of questions about his mother's kidnapping.

"The guys at school think you're really cool, mom," he said between bites of the sandwich Jenkins made for him. "They said their moms would fall to pieces if it happened to them."

Jenkins smiled. "Your friends might be surprised as to how their mothers would behave under similar circumstances." She poured Jason a glass of milk. "But enough about that. How would you like to go take the test for your motorcycle license?"

Jason's eyes widened. "Oh, mom! That'd be great."

She laughed. "Then let's get cracking."

"I gotta call Ross," Jason said the minute they returned. "I can't wait to tell him that I passed the test." He looked at Jenkins anxiously. "Could we get the motorcycle today?"

She shrugged. "If Ross says it's ready, I suppose so. But only after you've finished raking Mrs. Moody's yard."

"I'll do Mrs. Moody's yard as soon as I've called Ross."

Jenkins watched her son head for the phone. He'd kept his word about earning the motorcycle. In no time at all he had lined up jobs for every Saturday between now and Christmas and lined up even more during the Christmas holidays.

"Ross?" she heard Jason say into the phone. "Guess what! I've got my motorcycle license." Jenkins stood in the doorway of the kitchen hoping against hope that Ross would ask to speak with her. But a moment later, Jason hung up the phone.

Did he ask about me, she wanted to say. Instead, she simply said, "Well?"

"He said I could come get it anytime," Jason said excitedly. "He said he'd leave the key to it under the doormat."

"He won't be there?" She hoped her disappointment didn't show in her voice.

"Nah, he said he had some errands to run, but that I could go ahead and get it. Can we go, now, mom? Can we?"

Ross was obviously avoiding her. "What about the money?"

"He said not to worry, I could pay a little at a time."

"That isn't what I meant, Jason. I meant . . . never mind. I guess I can leave a check in his mailbox." She arched a brow at her son. "And you'll reimburse me as you get paid, right?"

"Sure. Don't worry, I won't renege on the deal." Jason looked at her expectantly. After a moment, he anxiously shifted his feet. "Mom, can we go now? He gave me directions. I know how to get there."

Jenkins ruffled her son's hair. When had he gotten so tall? "All right. Get your helmet and we'll go."

"Look, Mom, there she is!"

Jenkins, lost in thought, was startled by Jason's announcement. "W-who?" she stammered.

"The motorcycle, of course. Gosh, look how she shines!"

Jason leapt from the car the moment it stopped and hurried to retrieve the key under the doormat.

Shaking her head in amusement, Jenkins got out a moment later. "Don't you dare get on that thing without your helmet."

He grinned good-naturedly. "Yes, ma'am."

Jenkins opened her checkbook and tore out the one she'd written as a payment to Ross. She walked to the small front stoop and dropped it in the mailbox. As she turned to leave, she felt a prickling at the nape of her neck and looked behind her, half expecting to see him. But there was no one there. She looked at the window and thought she saw the curtain move slightly, but decided she must have imagined it.

"Let's go, mom!" Jason called as the engine thundered.

"All right, I'm coming," she yelled, but she

doubted Jason heard her over the roar of the motorcycle. She hurried to her car and got inside, then watched Jason ease the motorcycle down the drive and out into the street.

"Please, God," she murmured, "Watch out for my baby."

On Monday, Jenkins was sweeping her front walk when the familiar red sports car pulled up in front of her house. Her heart leapt when she saw Ross get out and walk toward her. She stifled the urge to check her hair with a quick pat.

"Hi," she said, nervously. "What brings you by?"

Ross reached into his back pocket and pulled out his wallet. "This," he said, taking out a folded slip of paper.

She took the paper and looked at it, then back at him. "This is the check I left in your mailbox. Isn't it the right amount?"

"Yeah, but I don't want your check. Jason is going to pay for the motorcycle from the money he earns. That was the deal."

"B-but that may take years, Ross," Jenkins argued. "It isn't fair to expect you to wait for your money. Jason can pay me."

Ross shook his head. "I don't need the money, Jinx. I wanted Jason to have the motorcycle. I would have given it to him, but he'll appreciate it more if he earns it."

Jenkins studied him. "I don't know what to say. Thank you doesn't seem like enough."

He shrugged. "It's enough."

"Oh. Well, um—would you like a cup of coffee?"

"No thanks. Kelly's waiting in the car."

"There's plenty of coffee if he wants some," she said.

Ross backed up a couple of steps and stuffed his hands in his back pockets. "Thanks, but we'd better get going. Kelly and I are working the day shift until after the first of the year, so we're on duty right now."

"Oh. Well, maybe some other time."

"Yeah, maybe," he said. Then he turned and strode to the car. He waved as the car pulled away from the curb.

Ross slumped down in his seat and stared grimly out the car window. "Sonofabitch," he muttered.

"What's eating you?" Kelly asked, glancing at him.

Ross shook his head. "Nothing." Then sighed. "I'm a fool."

Kelly grinned. "That's old news."

"She asked me in for coffee. She invited you, too."

"What's wrong with that?"

Ross looked at his partner. "That's just it, there's nothing wrong with it. But I said no." He stared out the window again. "You should have seen the look on her face. Like I'd slapped her."

Kelly was silent for a moment. "Look, Ross, if you—"

Ross held up his hand. "Drop it, Kelly. You made your point the other day and I listened. You were right. Jinx isn't the kind of woman who should get hooked up with somebody like me. It's better that I end it before somebody gets hurt."

The two friends rode in silence for several moments. Then, Kelly looked over at Ross. "If you ask me, it's too late."

Ross looked at him. "What do you mean?"

"I mean, partner, that from where I sit, it looks like you're hurtin' pretty bad."

Ross rested his head on the back of the seat and was silent for a moment. Then he said, "Better me than Jinx."

Jenkins scooped the last of the chocolate ice cream from the carton, stuffed it in her mouth, and shivered. She'd been weeping and eating ice cream since Ross dropped by to return her check, and now she was so chilled she didn't think she'd ever be warm again. She knew a hot shower would stop the chills, but the shower made her remember exactly what she was trying to forget.

She tossed the ice cream carton in the trash. Maybe a nice batch of brownies straight from the oven would warm her.

She opened a cabinet and began pulling down the ingredients. Yes, she'd make brownies, and if that didn't work, she'd try chocolate chip cookies, a pecan pie, and after that . . . cake. A big, three-layer chocolate cake with fudge icing. By the time she'd mended her broken heart, she'd probably have gained fifty pounds and developed a horrid case of acne, but so what? If it filled the hole in her heart, nothing else mattered.

She was reaching for the last brownie when Tish knocked on the back door. Jenkins motioned for her to come in, then picked up the brownie and stuffed it in her already full mouth.

"Oooh, do I smell brownies?" Tish asked.

"Mmmfufff," Jenkins said, pointing to the oven.

"You want to repeat that without food in your mouth?"

Jenkins swallowed and took a sip of coffee. "I said, the brownies are gone, but there are cookies in the oven."

"You ate a whole pan of brownies?"

Jenkins wiggled two fingers. "Two, and a gallon of chocolate ice cream."

"What are you trying to do, eat yourself into oblivion?"

Jenkins went to the oven and checked on the cookies. They weren't done, so she returned to her seat. "Let's just say I'm searching for nirvana."

"By eating everything in sight?"

"No, by eating every chocolate thing in sight." She picked up a crumb of brownie and popped it in her mouth. "They don't call it comfort food for nothing."

"And is this binge caused by Detective Handsome?"

Jenkins arched a brow. "How very astute of you."

"All right, out with it. What happened?"

"Nothing new. In my unique way, I managed to send him running for the hills." She laughed harshly. "I seem to annihilate any feelings a man might have for me. Maybe I was wrong to blame Jake for finding someone else."

"Oh, pish tosh," Tish said with a snort.

"Pish tosh?"

Tish grinned. "As my grandmother used to say. It

means, don't be ridiculous. You know very well that your ex-husband is an immoral, womanizing slug and the way he cheated on you was not your fault."

Jenkins nodded. "Yeah, you're right."

Tish sighed. "You look like hell, you know."

"You're a real friend, Tish."

"Well, you do. And only a true friend would tell you. Why don't you go take a nice hot shower and—Jenkins, what'd I say? Don't cry, honey, I didn't mean it when I said you looked like hell."

Sixteen

Poor Tish. Her guilt-ridden apologies turned Jenkins's sobs to giggles. "Oh, Tish, you didn't make me cry," she said, wiping away her tears. "I'm just having a pity party. I think it must be PMS."

"I still shouldn't have said you looked like hell."

"Why not? I do look like hell. And as you pointed out, only a friend would say so." She patted her friend's arm. "Tish, if you hadn't come over here I would probably have spent the rest of the day weeping and eating."

Tish looked at her watch. "Well, there's not much day left. It's after six o'clock."

Jenkins blinked. "It's that late? I had no idea." She slumped in her chair. "I guess I shouldn't be surprised. It takes a lot of time to eat a gallon of ice cream and make and eat two batches of brownies and bake two dozen chocolate chip cookies."

"Two dozen cookies?"

Jenkins nodded. "And I want you to take them home with you. I don't dare keep them in the house with the mood I'm in." She stood up. "I think I'll take your advice. I'm going to take a shower, put on some fresh clothes, and go to bed early. I'm sure when I wake up tomorrow I'll feel much better."

A few hours later Jenkins finally took Tish's advice. She took a shower in Jason's bathroom—she couldn't bring herself to go into the other one. She washed her hair, wrapped it in a towel and pulled on her robe. Then she padded barefoot into the den to watch television until she became drowsy enough to go to bed.

She was combing the tangles from her hair while watching an innocuous sitcom when the doorbell rang. She went to the front door, glanced at the grandfather clock in the entry hall and saw that it was after ten o'clock. She frowned. It was too late for salesmen or a casual visitor. She stood on tiptoe, peered through the tiny peephole, and saw Ross standing on the front porch.

"Ross?" Her hands were shaking, but she finally managed to unlock the door and open it.

He stepped inside, kicked the door shut, then took her by the elbow and began leading her toward the den. "We've got to talk," he said. When they reached the den, he pointed to the sofa. "Sit there."

Jenkins, nervously tugging the edges of her robe together, eased down to the sofa and tucked her feet under her. She looked at Ross expectantly. "W-what is this all about?"

Ross paced back and forth in front of the sofa.

"You know, don't you, that a cop is the worst person in the world to get romantically involved with?"

"No, I—"

"Cops are awful when it comes to relationships. Their hours are erratic, and sometimes, when there's a stakeout for instance, they have to be gone for days at a time. And I'm worse than most. I . . . cover your feet."

"What?"

"Cover your feet, they make me crazy."

"My feet?" She quickly pulled the hem of her robe over her feet.

"Yes, damn it, your feet. Don't you know you have the sexiest feet in the world?"

"I do?"

"Yes, you do." Jenkins had to force herself not to take a peek at her feet. No one had ever told her they were sexy.

"I can't help it, I'm nuts about your feet." He rubbed his hand over his face. "Oh, no, now I sound like a pervert." He shook his head. "I'm getting away from my point here. Let's get back to why I'm the wrong person for you."

He resumed pacing and Jenkins wondered idly if he were wearing a pattern in the rug. "A cop never knows if each day isn't going to be his last."

"Ross."

"It's really hard on their loved—"

"Ross!" Jenkins said sharply.

He stopped and looked down at her. "What?"

"Why are you telling me all this?"

"I'm telling you this so you'll show me the door and never speak to me again."

"Why?"

"I'm trying to make you see that getting involved with me would be the worse thing you could possibly do."

She studied him for a moment. "I don't understand."

He squatted so that his eyes were level with hers and his voice grew soft. "I shouldn't be here, Jinx. I'm lousy at relationships and I've never stayed in one for more than a month, at most. But I can't seem to stay away from you and that scares me to death."

She stroked his cheek. "Why does that scare you?"

"Because I'm afraid I'll end up hurting you. The other women I've had in my life have been just like me: out for a good time and that's all. Sometimes they were the first to end the relationship, and that was okay, too." He turned his face and kissed her palm. "But you're different, Jinx. You expect more, and damn it, you deserve more than a short-term affair. But knowing myself as I do, that may be all I'm able to give." He stood up. "So now that you know the way things are with me, you shouldn't have any problem sending me packing."

Jenkins patted the sofa beside her. "Sit down, Ross."

"Jinx, I don't—"

"Sit down," she said firmly. "I've listened to you, now it's your turn to listen to me."

He sat down beside her, but he didn't look at her. Instead, he rested his elbows on his knees and stared at the floor. She reached out and tugged sharply on his ponytail. "Look at me, Ross Tracy!"

"Ow! Okay!" He turned sideways on the sofa and faced her.

"Now, I want to get something straight, okay?"

He nodded.

"You're telling me that you want me to send you away because you can't do it yourself?"

"That's right."

"And this isn't some ploy just to get you off the hook?"

He frowned. "What?"

"I mean, do you swear that this isn't a way to get out of this relationship gracefully by allowing me to be the one to end it?"

"No! Of course not."

She arched a brow. "Temper, temper, Detective Tracy. I'm sorry if I've offended you, but I had to ask." She smiled slightly.

"I don't play games, Jinx."

She looked at her hands. "No, of course you don't."

He started to rise. "I guess I'd better get going."

"Ross, don't go, please."

He looked at her. "But I thought you understood."

Jenkins nodded. "I do understand, and your warning is duly noted."

"Now I don't understand."

She smiled. "I mean that I'm willing to take my chances with you, Ross Tracy. I'll take whatever you can give me for as long as you can give it. And when it's over, I'll remember that I was warned that it wouldn't last."

"Jinx." Ross shook his head and her name sounded like a plea. "This is crazy. You don't know what you're doing."

"I know exactly what I'm doing." She unfolded

one leg and placed a bare foot over his crotch. "Now then, tell me more about my sexy feet."

Ross chuckled and his bronze cheeks turned a trifle pink. He picked up her foot and ran his thumb along her instep. "I don't have a foot fetish, I swear I don't. I've never even thought about a woman's feet before. But your feet, well, they're just so damned feminine. They're so slender and . . . just look at this arch. Only a woman's foot could have an arch like this."

Jenkins felt herself becoming aroused. My God, she thought, I can't believe this. Ross's talking about my feet and it's turning me on! "Ross, I—"

"And look at these toes," he murmured, raising her foot to his lips. "They're perfect. Just the right size and shape for your foot." When he began kissing each toe Jenkins found she couldn't sit up anymore, so she lay back on the sofa and closed her eyes.

His large hands slid to her ankle. "I love your ankles, too," he said. "And your calves." His hand continued to move upward. "You have great knees, Jinx."

She swallowed and threw her arm over her eyes. "Do I?"

"Yeah, they have dimples. And I'm crazy about your thighs, especially this part here." He ran his fingers along the inside of her thigh and she trembled.

"Ross?" she said.

"Hmmm?" She felt the rasp of his whiskers against the inside of her knee.

"Are you going to get naked, or am I going to have to tear your clothes off myself?" When he didn't immediately reply, she lifted her arm and looked up at him. "Well?"

He grinned. "I sort of like the idea of your tearing off my clothes, but . . . since I don't have an extra wardrobe here, I guess I'd better take them off myself."

Jenkins watched through half-closed eyes as he stood up, kicked off his shoes, and peeled off his shirt. He dropped it to the floor and then reached for the button of his faded jeans.

Jenkins scrambled upright. "Wait, Ross. Put your shirt back on."

His hand froze on the button. "What's wrong?"

"Just put your shirt back on, please."

He picked up his shirt and shrugged it over his shoulders and began buttoning it. "Jinx, what's this all about?"

"I've never really seen you naked."

"Of course you have. What about the time—"

"I know there were times when I *should* have seen you, but the truth is that I've never had the chance to really look at you. It was kind of dark in the shower."

"What about—"

She shook her head. "That time I had my mind on Jason, remember? I could hardly see anything except what I was afraid he would see."

He narrowed his eyes suspiciously. "So what is it you want me to do?"

She spread her arms. "I want you to strip for me. I'll even provide music if you like."

Ross looked away for a moment. Then, with his fists on his hips, he glowered at her and growled, "All right, how did you find out? Who told you?"

She blinked up at him. "Who told me what?"

"You know what. Who told you?"

"Ross, honestly, I don't know what you're talking about."

"Nobody told you? Nobody told you how I supported myself in college?"

"No. How *did* you support yourself in college?" He simply stared at her and as understanding hit, her chin dropped to her chest. "You were a stripper?"

"Does that bother you?" he asked, watching her intently.

"No, it doesn't bother me. Why should it?"

He shrugged. "Some women might be bothered by it. It would bother me if you'd been a stripper."

She rose to her knees. "Ross, why would I be bothered by something you did in college? I assume you had a good reason for choosing that particular way to make a living."

He grinned crookedly. "Yeah, I had a good reason. The tips were a whole lot better than what I got waiting tables."

She let her gaze wander over him. "I'll just bet they were," she murmured, really studying his body: broad chest, narrow hips, long muscular legs, firm round—

"Jinx?"

She blinked and then laughed softy. "I'm sorry, I was just trying to imagine you on the stage taking your clothes off. Was I drooling?"

He chuckled and shook his head.

"Will you do your act for me?"

He crossed his arms. "No."

She frowned. "Why not? I've never seen a male stripper."

"Too bad. I'm not doing it."

"Spoilsport," she said petulantly.

Ross grinned and held out his hand. "Come here, Jinx." She rose from the sofa and took his hand. He bent, kissed her softly, and said, "I've changed my mind."

"About what?"

"About undressing. I'm not going to take my clothes off. If you want me naked, Jinx, you'll have to take them off me all by yourself."

Seventeen

Ross grinned as he watched her face grow faintly pink.

"So," she said, "You'll strip for hundreds of screaming women, but you won't strip for me?"

"That's right."

She shoved her hands in the pockets of her robe and smiled in a way that made the hair on the back of his neck rise.

"You don't think I can do it, do you?" she asked, walking slowly around him like a farmer checking out a mule he was thinking of buying. "You don't think I can undress you."

"Oh, I know you can do it," he said, swiveling his torso so that he could keep an eye on her. He didn't much like having her behind him, she seemed to be in a strange mood. "The question is," he continued, "will you dare?"

She made a complete circle and paused in front of him. "Oh, I'll do it, but there will be rules to this game."

"What kind of rules?" There was something in her eyes that make him wonder if he shouldn't change his mind and do the strip-tease after all.

She put her fingers on his shoulder and walked them across his chest, over his other shoulder and across his back, all the while circling him again. "Rule number one," she said softly. "You have to trust me."

He nodded. "That's easy. I do trust you."

She smiled that smile again. "Good. Rule number two: you have to do whatever I tell you to do."

"Now wait a minute—"

"Ah-ah-ahh," she admonished, covering his lips with her fingers. "You trust me, remember?"

"Yeah, but—"

"No buts. Either you trust me or you don't."

"I trust you."

"All right, here's rule number three: no matter what I do, you can't move unless I tell you to."

"I can't move?"

"Not a muscle." She stood back and crossed her arms. "Is it a deal?"

Ross thought for a moment. It sounded easy enough. Trust her, do whatever she told him, and don't move a muscle. The doing whatever she told him worried him some. With this strange mood she was in, she could make him do things he might later regret. "Jinx, you won't ask me to do something crazy, will you?"

She arched a brow. "Crazy like what?"

"Like go outside without my clothes?"

She covered her mouth and giggled. "No. Nothing like that. I promise."

"I'll go along with this game on one condition."

"And what condition is that?"

"A time limit. You have thirty minutes to do whatever you want with me, and then I have thirty minutes with you."

Jinx studied him, as if trying to decide. "We'll use the kitchen timer," she said.

Ross nodded. "Good idea, go get it."

Jinx ran to the kitchen and brought the timer into the den. She twisted the knob and set it for thirty minutes. Before releasing it, she looked at him. "Deal?" she asked.

He drew in a deep breath. "Deal."

She set the timer on a nearby table and he heard the ominous ticking. "Now, we begin." Jinx reached for the buttons on his shirt and slipped them loose very, very, slowly. She had to stand on her toes to slide the shirt off his shoulders and arms, but she finally managed and tossed it on a nearby chair.

"Very nice," she said, looking at him. She laid the flat of her hand on his chest and he flinched slightly. "Don't move a muscle," she said. "That was the deal."

"Couldn't help it," he murmured. "Your hand's cold."

"Oh, I'm sorry," she said, but her voice sounded anything but contrite. "Let's see if I can't change that."

Ross was wondering exactly how she meant to do

that when she reached both arms around him and pushed her hands into the back of his jeans. "Jinx!"

Jinx looked up at him with dancing eyes. "Just warming my hands, honeybuns."

He grinned down at her. "You could have given me some warning."

"Warnings weren't part of the deal," she said, squeezing his buttocks. He immediately felt himself harden. Ross knew then that it was going to be a long night.

"I think they're warm enough now, don't you?" she teased, slipping her hands out of his pants. "Now let's see if we can't get you out of these old things." Her fingers moved to the brass button at his waist and the moment her knuckles touched his stomach, he drew it in. "You're mov-ing," she said in a singsong voice.

"Haven't you ever heard of a knee-jerk reaction?" he said, suddenly finding it difficult to breathe.

"Yes," she said, "but I'm not anywhere near your knee." The button slipped loose and he heard the zipper slide downward. He knew his arousal had to be clearly evident by now and he wondered how Jinx was going to react to it. He didn't have to wait long.

"My, my, my, Detective Tracy," she said, as she tugged his jeans down over his hips. "You really are a big man in your jeans. These must be rather painful at times."

Ross smiled crookedly. "Yes ma'am, at times like this."

She followed the jeans down his legs and she knelt at his feet. "Lift your legs one at a time," she said, and he laughed. She looked up at him, perplexed.

"It would be hard to lift them at the same time."

Ross laughed again when she stuck her tongue out at him.

She slid her hands up his legs. "Let's see if you think this is funny." With those words her only warning, she grabbed his shorts and with a hard jerk, pulled them to his knees.

The breath went out of him. "Hey!" When she didn't say anything, he looked down at her and found she was staring at his fully erect manhood. "Jinx?"

She lifted her wide-eyed gaze to meet his questioning one. "My goodness, you're so . . . Do you have a condom?"

He closed his eyes and grimaced. Damn! "No."

"No?" He heard both disbelief and disappointment in her voice.

"Jinx, I didn't know I would need a condom. I came here expecting you to send me packing, remember?"

"Oh." She sat back on her heels and looked as if she were going to cry.

He started to kneel beside her and then caught himself. "May I move, please?"

She frowned up at him. "Why not? Game's over."

He kicked off his pants and got to his knees, facing her. Then he grinned. "I lied. I do have a condom. But it's in the car."

She crossed her arms and glared at him. "Ross Tracy, I'm appalled."

"Appalled? About what?"

"I'm appalled that you keep condoms in your car on the off chance that you . . . you . . . might get lucky."

"Jinx, I'm a single man. It would be appalling,

not to mention, irresponsible, if I *didn't* keep them."
She bowed her head and he put his finger under
her chin to raise her face. "Would it help matters
if I told you I haven't had the need of one since I
met you?"

Jinx gave him an embarrassed half-smile. "Yes."

"Will you let me get a condom from the car?"

Avoiding his gaze, she nodded. Ross stood up and
began pulling on his clothes. He suddenly seemed
to be all thumbs and had trouble buttoning his
jeans. He cursed under his breath and then Jinx
pushed his hands away.

"Let me," she said, her embarrassment seemingly
gone as she quickly slipped the brass button through
its hole. "There you go." She patted the bulge at
his fly and, eyes twinkling, she grinned. "I certainly
hope you don't lose your, er, resolve while you're
gone."

Ross chuckled. "Have no fear, Jinx. Where you're
concerned, I'm a man of firm and unfailing resolve."

Ross hurried out the door, cursing under his
breath as he stepped on pebbles with his bare feet.
After searching through a multitude of gas receipts,
packets of ketchup, paper napkins and a loan payment coupon book, he finally found what he was
looking for in the glove compartment of his car.
When he returned, he found the family room empty.

"Jinx?" he called.

"I'm back here."

Grinning, Ross strode down the hall to her bedroom. But when he got there, he still didn't find
her. "Jinx?" he said again.

"I'm in the bathroom." Ross moved toward the

closed door, but paused when she said, "I'll only be a moment."

He shrugged. "Okay." While he waited for her, Ross idly wandered around the room. He was curious about the things Jinx lived with. On the bedside table was a picture of Jason dressed in a basketball uniform. Next to the picture was a small silver box, and beside that was a pair of reading glasses atop a book. Ross moved the glasses and picked up the book. He frowned when he read the title: *How to Murder the Man of Your Dreams*. He looked toward the bathroom.

"Jinx? This book you've been reading—it isn't a how-to book, is it?"

She chuckled. "Of course not." And then, just as Ross opened the lid of the silver box, she added, " only murder snoops." He flinched guiltily, snapped the lid of the box shut and stuck his hands in his pockets.

"Hey you! I'm growing older by the minute," he said after several moments.

She laughed. "Good. If I stay in here long enough, maybe the next time I see you, you'll be as old as am."

Ross smiled and shook his head. "Let me put i another way. If I have to wait much longer, I could lose my . . . resolve."

The door to the bathroom flew open and Jenkins stuck her head out. "You wouldn't dare."

"I'm only human."

She stepped into the bedroom. "Did you get the condom?"

He held up the foil packet.

Jenkins's eyebrows rose. "That's it? You mean

you're going to put that teeny-weeny thing on your. . . ." She cleared her throat. "On yourself?" she finished, blushing furiously.

Ross fought a smile as he studied her. "Jinx, I have a feeling you've never seen a condom before. Am I right?"

She played with the belt of her robe. "Yes." Then she raised her chin and looked at him levelly. "The Pill was my contraceptive of choice back when. As for the other reasons for needing a condom. . . ." She lifted a brow. "If you'll recall, until quite recently I had no reason to be concerned about them."

"Well, Ms. McGraw," Ross said in a schoolteacher-ish tone, reaching for the button at the waist of his jeans. "I think it's about time you learned something new. Today we're going to study the prophylactic, or, as it's more commonly known, the condom."

He pulled off his jeans and sat down on the edge of the bed. He looked up then and saw to his amusement that she appeared to have turned to stone. "Come here, Jinx. The seminar I'm about to give is definitely meant to be a hands-on workshop."

Eighteen

Sunlight was streaming through the window when Jenkins blinked awake and rolled over to find Ross, sleeping deeply, nestled beside her. He must be exhausted, she thought, gazing at him. They'd made love until the wee hours of the morning and Ross had been the perfect lover: warm, gentle, and oh, so generous. He'd made her respond in ways she'd never dreamed were possible, took her to heights she'd never known existed. What she'd experienced with Ross last night was completely different from her much more ordinary sexual experience as Jake McGraw's wife.

"You were right, Ross," she whispered. "There really is a difference between making love and having sex."

Taking care not to disturb him, Jenkins slipped from the bed and pulled on her robe. She gathered up the clothes strewn about the floor, and then padded down the hall to the laundry room. After starting the first load of wash, she went in to make breakfast.

Ross awoke to find that Jinx had already risen. He heard the rattle of dishes and knew she was in the kitchen, probably making breakfast. He rolled to his back, put his hands behind his head, and stared at the ceiling. Last night had been incredible—and fun. God, he loved Jinx. She'd been so funny when he'd opened the foil packet and shown her the still-rolled comdom. She'd said it looked like a rain hat for an elf—and damned if it didn't look like one to him, too.

Ross's grin broadened. He'd never known a woman quite like Jinx. She'd actually made him laugh while they were making love. He couldn't remember anyone doing that before. Lovemaking had always been a serious business with him, even if he hadn't been exactly serious about his bed partners. But with Jinx it was . . . well, fun. As a matter of fact, everything about Jinx was fun and he imagined life with her would never be boring.

I could be happy married to a woman like Jinx,
e thought. Then he started. Married? Was he ac-
ually thinking about marriage? He waited for the
ttle voice in his head to tell him he was crazy, that
e wasn't meant to be married—but it didn't come.
or the first time in his life, marriage seemed plau-
ible—more than just plausible, with Jinx. As a mat-
er of fact, he might discuss that possibility with her.
amned if he wouldn't!

She was buttering the toast when Ross entered the
itchen. "Jinx, where in the hell are my clothes?"

Splendidly nude, Ross stood in the doorway look-
ng more beautiful than any work of art. "Good
morning to you, too," she said, enjoying the view.
Your clothes are in the wash."

He frowned. "And just what am I supposed to
ear while they're washing?"

"I sort of like what you're wearing now."

He leaned against the door frame and crossed his
rms. "Okay, I'll stay like this if you'll take off your
obe."

Frying bacon in the nude while hot grease popped
as not something Jenkins cared to try. "I have quite
nough spots, thank you very much, and I would just
s soon not add any to the mix. I'll find something
or you until your clothes are dry." She turned off the
urner. "I think I have something that will do."

Jenkins returned a moment later. "Here," she
aid. "See if this will fit."

Ross frowned at the huge, tent-like wrapper printed
ith large, pink roses. "You expect me to wear this?"
e groused.

"I'm afraid it's the best I can do. It belonged to
ake's Aunt Thelma who, luckily for you, is a rather

large woman. I just hope it'll fit across your shoulders. Please, just try it on."

Grumbling under his breath, Ross shrugged on the wrapper and fastened the buttons. It was snug through the shoulders, and the eyelet-trimmed hem stopped well above his knees, but it would suffice until he could put on his own clothes.

"Good God," he muttered when he looked down at himself. "If anybody sees me like this, I'll have to leave town."

Jenkins hid her smile behind her fingers. "Don' worry, Ross, nobody will see—"

"Yoo-hoo!" Tish waved through the window in the back door.

"Oh, brother!" Ross muttered, closing his eyes.

"I'm sorry," Jenkins said, giggling, and was rewarded with a glower from Ross. "I swear I didn' know Tish was coming by."

Jenkins went to the door and opened it. "Hi, Tish," she said, giving her friend a hug. "You're in time for breakfast."

"Just coffee for me, I ate breakfast hours ago."

"What brings you here this morning?"

"I thought you might like some company, but . . ." She arched a brow at Ross. "I see that you already have a visitor. I'm surprised at you, Jenkins."

Jenkins flushed and dropped her gaze. "Well, I—'

"You should have told me Aunt Thelma was coming for another visit." She moved in front of Ross and her twinkling eyes boldly inspected him from head to foot. "Gee, Aunt Thelma, you have extremely hairy legs. Maybe you should consider electrolysis."

"Very funny, Tish," Ross growled.

"Just a suggestion." Tish grinned and waved her hand. "That outfit is *you*, darling."

"Don't tease him," Jenkins said, trying not to giggle again. "He's already miffed because I put his clothes in the wash while he was sleeping."

"God, what I wouldn't give for a camera right now."

Ross glared at Tish. "If one word gets out—"

"My lips are sealed, Ross. Wild horses couldn't drag it out of me." Her eyes twinkled mischievously and she winked at him. "I promise, I'll never tell a soul about your feminine alter ego."

"I do not have an alter ego, feminine or otherwise, damn it!"

Jenkins laughed. "Ross, she's teasing you. Calm down." She gave Tish a stern look. "Enough, all right?"

Tish made an X over her chest. "Cross my heart and hope to die, I will never tell anyone that I saw you wearing Aunt Thelma's wrapper."

"Okay, guys," Jenkins said. "Breakfast is finally ready. Let's sit—"

The front door slammed. "Mom, you'll never guess what—" Jason stopped just inside the kitchen door and stared at the three adults staring back at him.

"Uh-oh," Tish mumbled.

Jenkins stepped in front of Ross as if her small frame could hide him from view. "Jason, what are you doing home in the middle of the week?"

Jason's wide-eyed gaze flicked from Ross to Jenkins and back. "There was a fire in the chemistry lab at school so they sent everybody home until next Monday. What's going on here?"

"W-we were about to have breakfast. Have you eaten?"

Jason ignored her question. "What's Ross doing here? And why's he wearing Aunt Thelma's robe?"

Tish rose from the table. "I think I'd better be going," she said quietly. She patted Jenkins's shoulder. "Call me?"

Jenkins nodded to her friend, and watched her slip out the back door. Then she turned her gaze back to Jason. "Ross's clothes are in the washing machine."

"Why?"

"Because they were soiled, honey. Come have some breakfast with us and tell us about the fire."

Jason crossed his arms. "Let me get this straight. You're telling me Ross came all the way over here just so you could wash the clothes that he was wearing?"

Jenkins fiddled with the tie of her robe. "No. He . . . he was . . . he was—"

"And to keep Ross company, you took off your clothes?"

Feeling incredibly stupid, and searching for the right words to explain, Ross pushed back his chair and rose from the table. "Jason," he said, "Your mother and I—"

"Ross, let me handle this," Jenkins interrupted sharply.

Ross sighed. "Jinx. Just tell him the truth."

"You don't have to tell me anything," Jason replied angrily. "I'm not a little kid, you know. I can see for myself exactly what's been going on between you two." He raised his chin and glared at Ross. "All this time I thought that you were *my* friend. Boy, was I a fool."

"I am your friend, Jason," Ross said, wondering

whether this poor kid was going to believe one word
he said. The added indignity of his wearing this old
lady wrapper was probably the last straw as far as
Jason was concerned.

Jason looked at his mother. "Tell me, mom, is this
your way of paying for the motorcycle?"

"Jason, that was uncalled-for," Ross warned, his
hands clenching into tight fists. "You owe your
mother an apology."

"It's all right, Ross," Jenkins said, glancing from
him to her son. "Jason didn't mean that. Did you?"

Jason's expression was one of pure disgust. "I
meant every word. You make me sick. Both of you
make me sick and I never want to see either of you
again!" He spun on his heels and headed for the
front door.

"Jason, wait!" Jenkins started after him, but Ross
caught her arm.

"Let him go, Jinx."

She jerked her arm, trying to get free of his grip.
"Let go of me, damn it! I've got to stop him."

"There's nothing you can say to him right now
that will make a difference. Give him some time to
cool down, and then when you talk with him, he
might listen."

She snatched her arm free and hurried toward
the door, but the rumble of a motorcycle engine
told her she was too late to stop him.

"Damn! Damn, damn, damn!" she sobbed. "I
wish he'd never gotten that motorcycle. There's no
telling where he'll go or what he'll do."

Ross walked up to her and without a word, gathered
her into his arms. "It's all right, Jinx," he soothed.
"When Jason cools down, he'll come back."

After a moment, Jenkins wiped her eyes. "Your clothes are probably dry by now, Ross. You might as well get dressed."

"I'll dress in a minute. Right now I want to make sure you're all right."

Her eyes filled with tears again. "Of course I'm not all right. How can I be all right? Good God, Ross, my son just all but called me a whore!"

"Listen, Jinx—"

"No! I don't want to listen. I want you to get dressed and get out of here. I don't want Jason to find that you're still here when he comes back—*if* he comes back."

Ross dropped his arms from around her and stepped back. "All right, I'll leave." He bent and kissed her brow. "I'll call you a little later, okay?"

She shook her head, avoiding his gaze. "Don't call me. Jason might answer the phone. It'll just cause more trouble."

Ross sighed heavily. "Will you call me, then?"

"Yes. Yes, I'll call you."

Jenkins walked into the living room and stared out the front window. Had Jason gone to his father? She hoped he had, and even more, she hoped Jake had been there for his son. Would Jason tell Jake about Ross and her? She sighed. Of course, he would tell him. And, as angry as he had been, he was sure to make it sound as sordid and tawdry as his fifteen-year-old mind was able.

"Jinx?" Jenkins turned to find Ross standing in the foyer. "I'm leaving now." She nodded. "You'll be all right?"

Jenkins closed her eyes. No, she wanted to scream.

I'm not all right, and I doubt I'll ever be all right again. But she said, "Yes. I'll be fine."

"You'll call Tish?"

She nodded again. "I'll call her." She turned back toward the window. "Please, go away Ross, I don't want your comfort right now."

Ross sighed heavily as he opened the door and then, almost as an afterthought, said, "Jinx, for what it's worth—I love you."

And before she could even comprehend, much less respond to his unexpected confession, Ross was gone.

Nineteen

Ross sat at his desk and stared at the phone, willing it to ring. He had a hunch where Jason might have gone, and he was hoping the call he was expecting would prove him right.

Ross rubbed his face. God, he was tired. It had been two days since Jason stormed out of his mother's house and that long since Ross had slept. He could only imagine what Jinx was going through. He longed to talk to her, to see for himself that she was all right. But she'd insisted that he not call. When he still hadn't heard from Jinx after twenty-four hours he called Tish. He remembered every word of their conversation.

"Jason hasn't returned, and Jenkins is out of her mind with worry."

"I'd better get over there," he'd said.

"Don't. I'm sorry, but seeing you will upset her more."

"She blames me, doesn't she?"

"She blames both of you. Jenkins is not thinking clearly right now. She's worried and scared. When things settle down, maybe the two of you can work this out."

Ross looked at the phone again. "Ring, damn it!"

As if by magic the phone trilled and Ross snatched up the receiver. "Tracy here," he rasped. He listened for a moment and smiled grimly. "I'll be there in an hour, Colonel March. Thanks."

Jenkins wiped her eyes as she spoke into the phone. "No, Jake, if I knew where he was, I wouldn't be asking if you'd seen him." She leaned her head against the wall. "I told you, he was angry with me and stormed out two days ago. I thought he might be with you. I didn't know you were out of town." She nodded, struggling not to cry. "Call me if you hear from him, okay?"

Tish put her hand on Jenkins's shoulder. "Jake hasn't heard from him, either?"

"No. He said he hasn't spoken with Jason since last Monday." Fresh tears filled her eyes. "Oh, Tish, where could he be?"

"I don't know, honey, but I'm sure that wherever he is, he's all right. If something happened, you would have heard by now."

Jenkins nodded. "You're right. I just wish he would call me, send me a note, anything, just so I'd know. . . ."

"I talked with Ross today."

She blew her nose. "How is he?"

"Concerned about Jason and worried sick about you. He seems to genuinely care for you, Jenkins. Why don't you call him?"

She shook her head. "I won't be seeing Ross again, Tish."

"Is that what you really want?"

Jenkins laughed bitterly. "Of course it isn't what I want. It's what Jason wants and Jason has to come first with me. I'm all he's got. It might be different if Jake were a good father. But even when we were married, Jake never had time for his son."

"I know. But it just isn't fair that you have to make all the sacrifices while Jake the Jerk does exactly as he pleases."

"Yeah? Well, who says life is fair?"

Ross eased his sports car through the front gates of Southern Military Institute and drove straight to the building designated as the Commandant's Office.

When he entered the small brick structure, Ross was met by a short, balding man with twinkling blue eyes and a handlebar mustache. "Colonel Marsh?"

SMI's Commandant of Cadets offered his hand. "That's right. And you must be Detective Tracy."

Ross shook his hand. "You said you'd found Jason McGraw?"

"Yes, sir. He was right where you predicted. I sent Captain Holmes to check on him—covertly, of course." The Colonel leaned back. "How'd you guess that he'd come here?"

"I tried to put myself in his place, tried to think

what I'd do if I were angry with my mother, and my father was as indifferent as Jake McGraw." Ross shrugged. "I figured that if there were a place near here where kids hang out, that's where Jason would go."

Colonel Marsh shook his head. "I was surprised when Mrs. McGraw called inquiring about Jason. He's a nice young man, not the sort who would run off like that. Or I didn't think he was."

Ross nodded. "Jason's a good kid. But he has some problems. I think once he talks rationally with his mom, things will work out for him. I just hope I can convince him of that."

"I hope so, too. I'm relieved that we know where he is." Colonel Marsh shook his head and smiled. "I would never have thought about the old fishing camp if you hadn't called. I should have, because it's a perfect spot for someone looking to hide out a while. The lake's full of bass, there's an artesian well with the sweetest water you've ever tasted, and there's even a shack with a wood stove and a cot—a veritable paradise for a boy."

Ross stood. "Well, Colonel, I'd like to go out there and try to talk with Jason."

Ross hiked up the trail to the lake. He moved quietly, knowing that Jason would probably run the moment he saw him. As angry as he was for the things Jason had said to Jinx, Ross couldn't help but feel a little sorry for him. It had to have been pretty rough on the kid finding out about him and Jinx the way he had. No kid ever liked the idea of his mom allowing someone other than his father into her bedroom. If only Jinx had talked with Jason honestly about the two of them, this mess could have been avoided—maybe. Of course, Ross conceded, it might have happened anyway. When it came to teenagers, there was no telling how they would react.

Ross topped a rise and paused when he saw the shack Colonel Marsh had mentioned. He scanned the perimeter, looking for any sign of Jason, and spotted him fishing at the edge of the lake. "Okay," Ross murmured, "Here goes nothing."

He had gotten within eight feet of Jason before the boy saw him and ran. "Jason, wait!" Ross called, and then grumbled an exasperated, "Damn it!" as he took off after him.

Jason was no match for a man who'd been trained to chase fleeing felons, and Ross quickly tackled him to the ground.

"Let me go, you big jerk!" Jason yelled, kicking and fighting with all his strength—which was considerable for such a wiry-looking kid. They rolled through the dirt, but Ross held fast, wrapping both his arms and legs around Jason.

"Listen to me, Jason," Ross panted. "We can do this one of two ways. You can walk back to the shack like a man, or I can hog-tie you and carry you back like an animal. The choice is yours."

"I'll walk," Jason growled. "Just get off me."

"All right, I'm going to let you get up. But if you run again, I'll catch you. And the next time I won't give you a choice. You got that?"

"Yeah, I got it. Just let me get up."

Ross released his hold and got to his feet. He offered a hand up to the boy, but Jason ignored it and strode toward the shack. "Round one," Ross muttered as he trudged behind him.

"How'd you find me?" Jason asked the moment they entered the shack. "And what the hell do you want, anyway?"

Ross pulled up a wooden crate and sat down, motioning for Jason to do the same. "I'm an expert at finding people who don't want to be found. And I think you know what I want."

"Why don't you tell me, anyway," Jason retorted sullenly.

"I came to take you home."

"Well, you've wasted your time, 'cause I'm not going."

"Your mother's worried sick about you."

Jason looked at Ross, his face a mask of contempt. "I'm sure you can make her feel better." He spat on the floor. "I should think you'd be glad to see me gone. That way you and my mom could have the place to yourselves without interference."

Ross sighed. "Jason, your mother loves you. Don't you know that you mean more to her than anyone else in the world? There is nothing she wouldn't do for you, nothing."

"Oh, yeah?" he sneered.

"Yeah. And there's nothing I wouldn't do for your mom." Ross swallowed. "And that's why I'm not going to see her anymore."

That statement seemed to have gotten Jason's attention. He looked at Ross. "What do you mean?"

"Just what I said. If my presence is going to cause trouble between you and your mom, then I'm backing out."

"What does mom think about that?"

"She agrees. She loves you and since her relationship with me obviously hurts you, we'll end it."

Ross rested his elbows on his knees and leaned forward. "Don't you see, Jason, that's what love is all about? When you love somebody, really love them, you do whatever you can to make them happy. And if it means sacrificing something that's important, then you'll do that, too." Okay, Ross thought, so I'm laying it on a little thick. But I'll say whatever it takes to get this kid to let me take him home without a struggle.

Jason picked up a twig from the floor of the cabin and snapped it in two. "I thought you were *my* friend," he said, quietly. "And all the time you were just sniffin' around my mom."

Ross sighed and shook his head. "Jason, I love your mom, but I like you, too, whether you believe it or not. I had hoped that you and I could pals. I'd even hoped that we could become a family someday."

Jason appeared to be listening, so Ross pressed on. "You and I have a lot in common, you know? Like motorcycles, for instance, and baseball. I'd even bought us tickets to a Braves game."

Jason rubbed the toe of his sneaker in the dust. "My dad would take me if he had time," he said. "He's just too busy, with his business and all." He looked up at Ross. "My dad loves me, Ross, he's just real busy."

Ross's heart turned over at the pain he saw in Jason's eyes. Jake McGraw had to be a fool not to recognize what a terrific son he had. "Of course your dad loves you. I never doubted it. You're a great kid and he'd have to be stupid not to know it."

Jason chewed his lip and looked out the window. "Mom's really upset, huh?"

"Yeah. Tish says she's been crying ever since you left."

Jason looked at his feet again. "I didn't mean to make her cry. I was just so mad when I saw you with her. And then I knew that you two were . . . well, you know what I knew."

Ross nodded. "We should have talked with you and told you how we felt about each other. It wasn't something we planned. I'm not even sure how it happened, but it did. The only thing I regret is that you found out the way you did."

"I felt betrayed. All these weeks you've been—"

"No, not for that long, Jason. Your mom and I were merely friends until just recently. Neither of us would admit to our feelings at first. I was afraid of commitment, she was afraid of hurting you."

"So what changed things?

"The day Ray Price took your mother hostage made me realize how much I cared for her." He ran a hand over his eyes. "Jeez, I was scared to death that I was going to lose her."

Jason grimaced. "I said some pretty awful things to her."

Ross stared at the dirt floor beneath his feet and nodded. "Yeah, you did. I've never seen anyone so hurt by words."

Jason scratched his arm. "Think she'll forgive me?"

Ross raised his gaze to the boy's worried face. Then he grinned and reached over to ruffle Jason's hair. "I think so."

Jason looked at his watch. "I guess we'd better get

started if we want to get home before dark. Where'd you park your car?"

Ross stood up and dusted off his jeans. "By the road."

"No kidding? You hiked all the way here?"

"What's the big deal? Isn't that how you got here?"

"Yeah."

"Great. Then we can hike back together. You game?"

Jason grinned from ear to ear. "Heck, yeah. Let's go."

"Ross?" Jason said, as they walked back down the hill.

"Yeah?"

"Did you mean what you said back there?"

Ross glanced at Jason. "Which part?"

"The part about wantin' us to be like a family."

"Yeah, I meant it. Why?"

"I just wondered." Jason walked a little farther and then said, "So, are you gonna ask my mom to marry you?"

Ross glanced over at Jason. "Do you want me to ask her?"

Jason shrugged. "I guess I wouldn't mind if you did."

Ross studied him for a moment. "I'll tell you what, Jason," he said. "We'll leave it up to your mom. How about that?"

"What do you mean?"

"I mean," Ross said, "if your mom wants to marry me, she can do the asking."

Jason just stared at him. "You mean mom's gotta do the proposing?"

"That's right."

"But what if she won't do it?"

It was Ross's turn to shrug. "Well, if you really meant what you said about your mother and me, then I guess it'll be up to you to convince her, pal."

Twenty

Jenkins had finally given in to Tish's nagging that she get some sleep. She was lying on the sofa trying not to imagine all the things that could have happened to her son when she heard the sound of a now-familiar engine. She sat up and listened. "Did you hear that?"

Tish cocked her head. "Yeah, sounds like a car in the driveway."

"Oh my God!" Jenkins gasped. "That's Ross's car." She jumped up and headed toward the front door. "Maybe he's found Jason."

Hands shaking with excitement, Jenkins fumbled with the locks on the front door, threw the door open and stepped outside. Tish followed.

Jenkins was overjoyed to see her son—and Ross. She ran toward them, as Jason got out of the car and came around to meet her.

"Hi, mom," he said, as Jenkins threw her arms around him.

Laughing and crying at the same time, Jenkins pulled her son into a tight embrace and kissed every inch of his face. Then she looked over his shoulder at Ross, who stayed in the car.

Thank you, she mouthed. Ross gave her a mock salute, and Jenkins watched as he drove out of her life.

Good-bye, Ross, she said silently. Then blinking back her tears, Jenkins hugged her son. "I'm so glad you're home, Jason," she murmured. "Please don't ever run away like that again."

Jason looked at his shoes and nodded. "I won't, mom. I'm really sorry that I said those awful things to you."

"I know, darling, and I forgive you. Let's put all that behind us, okay? You need to tell your dad you're home."

Jason nodded, clearly relieved.

With her arm around his shoulders, Jenkins led her son toward the house. "How on earth did Ross find you, Jay?"

Jason grinned. "He's a detective, mom. He's trained to find people who don't want to be found. He's smarter than me and you put together."

"True enough," she murmured.

"Jinx, for what it's worth—I love you." Jenkins stared out the window as she remembered Ross's words. She sighed. If he loved her, why hadn't he called? Why hadn't he come to see her? It had been over a week since she'd heard from him. She sighed again when she heard the buzzer on the dryer go off and she turned away from the window.

"I'll get them, mom," Jason called.

"Thanks, sweetie." Jenkins smiled. Jason had changed so much since coming home, and much of the change was Jake's doing. When Jenkins called her

ex-husband to tell him Jason was home, Jake came
over immediately. Finally, the three of them were able
to have a long-overdue talk about the future. Jenkins
had been gratified by the way Jake had handled the
situation. He had gently, but firmly told Jason that he
had to accept that his parents were divorced and that
the situation wasn't going to change.

To Jenkins's surprise and relief, Jason accepted
Jake's words with a maturity she'd not witnessed in
her son before. Jake must have noticed it to, because
when he left that evening, he promised to spend
more quality time with his son.

Jenkins walked into the den. "Mom," Jason said
when she sat down beside him. "Have you heard
from Ross lately?"

She shook her head. "No." She began folding a
shirt.

Jason added a T-shirt to the growing stack. "You
know," he said, quietly, "Ross and I talked the day
he brought me home."

"Did you?"

"Yeah. He told me some stuff about you and
him."

Jenkins paused and looked at her son. "What kind
of stuff?"

Jason shrugged. "Oh, about how loving somebody
sometimes means sacrifice. He said that you loved
me and that you'd sacrifice everything to keep me
happy."

Jenkins swallowed and looked down so that Jason
wouldn't see her tears. "He's right, I would. You mean
everything to me."

Jason nodded. "Yeah, Ross said the same thing
about you."

"I don't understand what you mean?"

"Ross said he loves you and would stay away because of it."

Jenkins turned to face Jason. "Ross said he was going to stay away *because* he loves me?"

"Yeah. Well, I can't remember his exact words, but he said something like that." Jason shook his head. "Ross said something else, too, but I didn't think he meant it." He sighed heavily. "But I guess he did."

Jenkins stared at her son. "What else did he say?" Jason avoided her gaze and shrugged. Jenkins shook his shoulder. "Jason McGraw, if you don't tell me what else Ross said, I'm going to pour sugar in the gas tank of your hog!"

Ross fingered the heavy vellum of the engraved invitation.

"What's that?" Kelly asked.

"It's an invitation to a birthday bash for Tish Armstrong." He tossed it to Kelly. "It's at La Petite Fleur."

Kelly looked at it and whistled. "Says it's black tie. Pretty fancy for you, Tracy." He arched a brow. "Are you going?"

Ross grinned. "What do you think?"

Kelly chuckled. "I think you're going, black tie and all."

Ross resisted the urge to pull on his collar as he handed the maître d' his invitation. He avoided the eyes of La Petite Fleur's diners as he followed the man through the large dining room to a private one. The room was empty and Ross looked at the maître d'. "Are you sure this is the right room?"

The man bowed slightly. "Yes, sir. The other guests should be arriving shortly." And before Ross could ask anything else, the man was gone. He gazed about. It wasn't very large as dining rooms go. And, except for one small table in the center, it was empty. It certainly didn't look like a room where there was to be a birthday party. Where were the balloons, he wondered absently, and the colored streamers? Where was the birthday cake?

"Hello, Ross."

Ross spun around and saw Jinx smiling from the doorway. She was dressed in a cinnamon-colored strapless gown that clung to her curves and stopped at her ankles. Though he couldn't see the gold of her eyes from where he stood, he knew exactly how they looked. He ought to, he'd seen them often enough in his dreams.

As if he were still dreaming, Ross moved toward her. "Jinx," he said. He wanted to say more, but his throat was dry as dust and his lips wouldn't form the words. Hell, he couldn't even think, all he could do was stare at her.

"You're looking well."

"You, too," he finally managed. He cleared his throat. "We seem to be the first ones here."

She smiled. "Why don't we sit down?"

Ross wondered if they should sit at the only table in the room. Wouldn't it be reserved? Who cares, he thought. He'd sit in the street naked if that's what Jinx wanted. He pulled out a chair for Jinx and took the other across from her.

"How've you been?" he asked, drinking in the sight of her.

"I've been well," she said. "And you?"

"Fine. Just fine." He drew in a breath. "How's Jason?"

"He's great. Back at military school."

Ross nodded. "Good, good." He leaned forward. "Jinx, I—" Just then a waiter arrived. "Would you care to order now?" he asked.

Ross opened his mouth to tell him they were there for a party, when Jenkins said, "Yes, please. We'd like the Beef Wellington." She glanced at Ross. "Is that all right with you, darling?"

Ross blinked. She'd called him darling! "What about the other guests?" he asked when the waiter was gone.

"There are no other guests, Ross."

"What? But I thought—"

Jenkins smiled. "Listen. Do you hear that?" Ross cocked his head and listened and from somewhere in the building he heard soft music playing. "Shall we dance, Detective Tracy?"

Ross pushed back his chair and stood up. "I'd be honored, Mrs. McGraw," he said, offering her his hand.

He drew her into his arms and closed his eyes as they swayed to the hidden music. "What's this all about, Jinx?" he asked, kissing her ear.

She looked up at him. "I wanted tonight to be special," she said.

"Why?"

She wrinkled her nose at him. "Stop being a detective for a moment and just enjoy the evening."

"All right, I will." He nestled his face in her neck

and she giggled softly. "God, Jinx," he murmured. "You smell good."

"So do you." Then she laughed. "Déjà vu all over again, isn't it?"

They continued to dance until their dinner was served. The Beef Wellington was probably good, but it might just as well have been cardboard as far as Ross was concerned. He never even looked at what he was eating because he couldn't bear to take his eyes off Jinx.

When the table was cleared, Jinx asked, "Would you like dessert?"

He reached across the table and took her hand. "Yes. I want you for dessert. Let's get out of here."

"Not yet," she said, mysteriously. "There's something I want to give you." She opened her evening bag and took out a small velvet box. Smiling, she placed it on the table in front of him.

"What is this?" he asked.

"Open it and see for yourself."

Puzzled, Ross picked up the box and examined the outside of it. Then, still puzzled, he looked at Jinx. "Go on," she said. "Open it."

He raised the hinged lid. There on the satin lining, a diamond stud winked up at him. Ross looked at Jinx, totally confused. "I don't understand," he said.

"Don't you recognize an engagement earring when you see one?" she asked.

Ross swallowed. "An en-engagement earring?"

Jenkins reached over and took his hand. "Jason told me that you said if I wanted to marry you, I'd have to do the proposing. So here goes." She took a deep breath. "Ross Dylan Tracy, will you do me the honor of becoming my husband?"

"Have you talked this over with Jason?"

"Who do you think gave me the idea for this romantic rendezvous?" Jenkins laughed softly. "So what's your answer, Ross? Will you marry me?" He didn't reply, and Jenkins's voice wobbled just a bit when she said, "Ross?"

"I'm thinking," he replied.

"You're thinking!" Her tone held a touch of annoyance. "I've gone to all this trouble to propose and you have to think about your answer?"

He raised a brow. "Do I have to take your name?"

She stared at him, and saw that his eyes were twinkling. "No, I thought I'd take yours. Jenkins Tracy has a nice ring to it, don't you agree?"

"Definitely." He crossed his arms. "Okay."

"Okay, what?"

"Okay, I'll marry you."

Jenkins grinned. "You will? You're sure about this?"

Ross rested his elbows on the table and smiled at her. "Jinx, I have never in my life been as sure about anything as I am about spending the rest of my life with you."

"Oh, Ross!" Jenkins jumped up from her chair, and grinning from ear to ear, Ross opened his arms, expecting her to rush into them. His grin slipped when she ran right past him.

He turned in time to see her fling open the door of the dining room and yell at the top of her lungs, "He said yes, everybody!"

In the next moment, people began to fill the empty room. Ross looked around, stunned to see that quite a few of the grinning faces belonged to his friends from the police department.

Patrolman Ed Patches grabbed Ross's hand and pumped it. "Looks like you're gonna be tied to the little lady for the rest of your life, Ross. Who woulda believed it was gonna turn out like this?"

Ross smiled at the older man. "Yeah, I found I liked hanging out with her," he quipped, and Ed laughed and pounded him on the back. Tish was next in line to congratulate him.

"I swear, Ross Tracy, I thought you looked good in your street clothes, but in a tux you're absolutely devastating. Don't you agree, Buzzy?"

"I'd say he looks quite dapper," Buzzy replied, reaching to shake Ross's hand. "Congratulations, Ross. Tish and I are pleased for both of you."

"Thanks, Buzzy, I appreciate the sentiment." Then he turned and swung Tish into his arms. "And as for you," he kissed Tish noisily on the cheek, "that's for being such a great friend."

"You're more than welcome, Detective Hunk, I was happy to oblige. Now put me down before Jenkins becomes insane with jealousy and attacks me."

Ross grinned. "Do you think she'd do that?"

"I might," Jenkins said, winking at Tish.

In the next instant, Kelly pulled Ross into a bear hug. "Congratulations, partner. You're a lucky guy."

"You're right about that," Ross said, grinning.

"I thought I'd bust a gut when you got that invitation. I was afraid you were going to refuse when I saw that look on your face."

Ross stared at Kelly. "You knew? You knew what this was about the day I got the invitation?"

Kelly laughed. "Oh yeah, I knew. Hell, we all knew. Jason's been planning this thing for days."

"Where is Jason?"

Jason, who'd been hovering nearby, stepped up beside Kelly, "Here I am, Ross. You said I'd have to convince mom to propose, but it didn't take much convincing at all. She wanted to call you immediately, but I told her this way would be more fun." He held out his hand to Ross. "Congratulations, Ross. I'm real happy that you're gonna be my stepdad."

Ross ignored the outstretched hand and pulled Jason into his arms. "Thanks, Jay," he said, as tears stung his eyes. "I'm real proud that you're going to be my stepson."

Jenkins walked up beside Ross and Jason. "I think, Detective Tracy, that's it's time you did your part in tonight's celebration."

Ross looked. at her, puzzled. "My part?"

"Yeah, you know. I proposed and now you're supposed to do your part."

Ross grinned. "Oh, *my* part," he said, taking her in his arms. "The kissing part."

"Yeah," Jenkins said, just before his lips closed over hers. "And I expect you to do your part every single day for the next fifty or so years."

"Sounds like a plan. Let's get started."

And that's exactly what they did.

ABOUT THE AUTHOR

For eighteen years, Sabrah H. Agee was employed as an office manager/investigator for Alabama's largest judicial circuit. Since her job presented her with the sordid side of life, she began to write romances—stories that always had happy endings—as a means of coping. Sabrah received a lucky break when friend and fellow writer Beverly Barton introduced her to the Heart of Dixie Chapter of Romance Writers of America. For the past five years, Sabrah has driven three hours each month to attend meetings with other romance writers—many of whom she counts as her dearest friends. Sabrah says that joining Heart of Dixie was the smartest thing she ever did because "nobody understands a writer like another writer."

Sabrah and Kit, her best friend and husband of thirty-one years, make their home in Alabama, and you can write to her at P.O. Box 997, Selma, AL 36702.